THE
RAMBLING

Also by Jimmy Cajoleas
Goldeline

THE
RAMBLING

JIMMY CAJOLEAS

HARPER
An Imprint of HarperCollinsPublishers

Library of Congress Control Number: 2018939979
ISBN 978-0-06-249878-6

Typography by Katie Fitch
19 20 21 22 23 PC/LSCH 10 9 8 7 6 5 4 3 2 1

First Edition

I

IT WAS AFTER MIDNIGHT ON my eleventh birthday when I snuck out of Mom's house and hit the road on the search for my daddy. I packed me a knapsack with some bread and cheese and an apple. I left Mom a note saying, "Sorry, the fire was an accident like I told you it was, I've gone to live with Pop, love you, and may our paths cross again someday soon if the Fates should wish it," which I thought was a pretty nice touch.

I waited till the darkest, blackest time of night, when ugly gray clouds drowned all the moonlight. I snuck right out through my window, didn't wake a soul, dropped down to the earth, and got to moving. I was headed right out of Collardsville, I was, right out of the dirty dull town, taking that muddy moonless road down south.

I hadn't seen Pop in five years, but last I heard he was bunking somewhere down river, near the swamp where I was born and raised, back when he and Mom were still together, back when we were a family. I was going to live with him, same as I always dreamed of doing since we first moved away from him, away from the waters and the swamp, up into town. No more being the town flunky, no more being the shame of my mom. I was on to new things now, to take my place right alongside Pop, who was my hero, one hundred percent, not a doubt in my mind. I was so excited I figured my heart would burst right out of my chest and go running ahead of me.

Pop was something else, I'm telling you. A true wild man, the likes of which were disappearing off the face of this world just as fast as every unmapped forest. Pop was a master of a million arts—a poet, a carpenter, a pugilist of the highest order, and (I had been told) the handsomest man in twelve counties. So what if he was always too busy to come visit me? Why would he, with us living in the town like this, the dirty cluttered cobblestoned roads, boring and respectable, full of fences and gates and doors with locks on them, where a wild soul like Pop couldn't find any freedom or peace?

I loved Mom, quiet and strong as she was, even if she was always harsh on me, even if I couldn't hardly make it through one day without getting punished for something dumb, something bad I didn't even mean to do, it was only my old foul luck getting me in trouble all the time. Mom smelled like eggs and yeast and flour, and every time she hugged you, your clothes got dusted white. But Mom wanted me to become a baker like her. No way in Heaven or Hell was I going to sit in some hot room all day rolling dough. No sir, I knew it in the deep downs of my heart. It was the open road for me, the dusty trail, and best of all the long snaky sneaking river that slithered its way down to the Swamplands, the place Pop most loved, whose waters I'd been born and raised on until I was six and that Pop still wrote me about whenever he was able to write. It was the swamp I missed most of all.

Besides, I couldn't stay in town. Not after what I'd done.

Or at least, what Mom thought I'd done.

It was a long journey I was headed on, let me tell you. Tough too. Wished I could have taken a dirigible like I'd seen float over us once at the county fair. Rides on it cost more than Mom makes in a whole year. Another reason to leave this dopey town.

Nope, instead I walked.

I walked and I walked and I walked.

All night I walked, and come morning I took to hitchhiking. I rode a blind donkey and a bald horse (the owner said he lost his mane in a fight). I rode in a fancy lady's carriage

("Oh you poor thing!" she said) until she got a whiff of how I smelled and made me ride up top with the driver, which was fine with me.

Never had I seen so much of the country, even if it was mostly ugly old farmers wandering through their corn. It took days and days of dreary walking, constant traveling, bumming rides, and sleeping under trees on the side of roads. I kept hoping something wild would happen, something exciting, like maybe I would get robbed or see a ghost or get attacked by wolves. But naw, it was just a long bumpy journey, same as always. I slept under wagons and up in trees and in the tops of barns, always with my eyes open, always looking, looking, looking.

The fields became woods and the ground got murkier, and it was hard, hard to get a ride.

I took up with a fearful old codger on a mule. He slouched and had a beard that grazed his belly. His eyes were bright gold behind his spectacles and he rode all night, barely faster than I could walk.

"What are you so worried about?" I said.

"The Creepy," he said, "lives in the swamp, he does. Eats babies right out of their moms' cribs. Likes to gnaw on dead bones."

"We ain't even in the swamp yet," I said. "We're miles and miles from any notion of a swamp."

"Try telling that to the Creepy."

That night we slept tired and mosquito-bit on the side of the road, and when I woke up my shoes were gone. The old man sat there, chewing on some bread.

"What happened to my shoes?" I said.

"The Creepy," he said, and spat.

Truth was, I was happy to be on the journey, no matter how bad it was. I'd already run away a dozen times, but I always came back because I knew me leaving would break Mom's heart. Besides, she needed help in the bakery. I only ever left for a day or so at a time. So now that I'd gone and wrecked everything, I figured Mom was lucky to be quit of me. I was happy I wouldn't be a nuisance to her anymore. Because let's face it, I was no good as a baker. In fact, I wasn't much good at anything. If you accused me of being a bad kid and a no-good son, well, you wouldn't be too far off the mark.

I will not lie, I was a rambunctious child. I'd ruined pastries, burned tarts, sold moldy rolls to old ladies. I'd stolen a new rabbit coat just to get caught with it. I'd skipped chapel and chipped my tooth on the holy cup. I'd joyridden on neighbors' stallions and climbed to the top of the schoolhouse with an old pirate's spyglass just to see what I could see. I back-talked, spat in public streets. I left the house at all hours and spent my nights with the cows in the pasture up under the big bright moon. Harmless stuff, really, if you want to know the truth about it.

But I had another thing working against me too, and that was my durn horrible luck. For instance, I'd been thrown off no less than six horses, even broke my arm once. I'd contracted whooping cough and pleurisy and hay fever and summer chills and winter fever. I got myself thrown out of school for pushing my teacher down the stairs, but I swear to you it was an accident. I tripped, I did, stumbled right over my own two feet and there was Miss Halloran right in front of me, and I reached out to get a hold of something and down she went. She didn't hardly turn her ankle—it was only three steps down to the grass—but it was enough to get me tossed. Then there was the time Mr. Disley the Potter's wagon tipped and all his oxen got free and his entire stock got smashed and shattered, not a single pot left intact. You don't even want to hear about that one. Rest assured I was innocent entirely. Rest assured not a single person in the village—even my own mom—believed me.

It's embarrassing, all that bad fortune, when your daddy is a famous Parsnit player, renowned for his lucky blood. Why didn't I get that lucky blood, huh? If I had Pop's heart like Mom was always telling me (that's what she said when I did something wrong or got in trouble: "I hoped you'd have my heart at the bottom of it all, Buddy. But nope, you got your daddy's heart. You're your pop's child, through and through"), why didn't I get his lucky blood too? Everything I put my hand to wound up a disaster. So you can understand why perhaps I didn't see much benefit in being good, since it got fouled up every time anyway.

But set the bakery on fire?

That I did not do, I swear to you on a stack of holy books, cross my heart. I did *not*. It just happened.

See, it was early morning and I couldn't sleep.

Mom should have been up already, tending the oven, getting the fires going so they'd be good and hot for the bread. But when I tiptoed into Mom's bedroom, she looked so calm, so peaceful, like she was relaxed for once, not mad or sad or worried about anything. It was like she was smiling almost, and it had been ages since I'd seen her smile. I had seen her up late nights, near to dawn light, cooking up something in the bakery. Whenever I asked her about it, she just said, "Working on a new recipe. Something that will really change stuff for you and me, Buddy." And then she'd put her head down and get back to work. I knew Mom was tired, wore out to the bone. I figured maybe I could get the fires going for her, let her sleep a little bit longer. Everybody knows half an hour's extra shut-eye in the morning is about the best thing there is, especially for a person who works as hard as Mom.

So I went out back to the kitchen, where we kept the two big brick ovens that Mom did all her baking in. It was connected to a storefront where we sold everything.

I pulled up the wood and I lit the kindling and I got the

fire going pretty good. I was poking around with a stick, shoving the coals, making sure the air could get to all the logs, when I happened to glance out the window.

That's when I saw the toad. It was huge, like longer than my forearm, even hunched over, sitting like that. It was the biggest toad I'd ever seen in my whole life. I bet its legs were three foot long each, fully extended.

I know, right? What was a foot-long toad doing in town? What was it doing dry and miles off from any water, croaking away on my windowsill?

It blinked at me.

I realized it only had one big baby-blue eye staring at me, right in the center of its forehead. Must have been hexed. I crossed myself six times and spit like you're supposed to.

That toad stared and stared.

I felt dizzy, strange, like I needed a glass of water, like I'd better sit down.

I'm not sure what happened after that. I guess I blacked out. Because when I came to, the stick I was poking the fire with had caught, and it was leaning against a pile of old empty flour sacks Mom had left lying around.

I don't need to tell you the whole thing was already blazing.

I tried to put it out. I *did*. But before I could make much of a dent in it, Mom came running in, screaming.

"Put it out, Buddy!" she hollered. "Oh Lord God in

Heaven help us, you lit the bakery on fire!"

Mom came back with a bucket of water and a big old blanket. The fire wasn't huge, and the bakery was built pretty sturdy with brick. A couple of the neighbors had run in to help (you know how that word *fire!* can spread faster than the flames themselves). Only half the bakery burned down. It didn't even reach the upstairs, where we lived, where Mom had been sleeping. I counted that a blessing, I did.

'Course I couldn't find the toad that had mesmerized me with his one jeweled eye, and when I tried to tell Mom about it, all she did was mutter to herself, like I wasn't even there.

"I have had all I can stomach," whispered Mom, tears rolling down her cheeks. That was a big deal, and it scared me a little. Never before had I seen my mom cry. She was tough, she was, and quiet. The most you'd ever get out of her was a little chuckle here and there, or a straight-line kind of frown. "I try and I try and I try, and nothing works. I can't even sleep in an hour without it all coming to ruin."

"But Mom," I said. "There was this toad . . ."

Mom shushed me.

"It ain't worth arguing about, Buddy," she said. "Not now. But rest assured, you and me are going to have us a talk tomorrow, and I'm afraid you won't like what you're going to hear."

I'd be a liar if I said that didn't hurt. In fact, it hurt so bad I knew there was no way I could stay at home any longer, not the way I always wrecked things, not how hard I made Mom's life. It hurt me to leave, especially on my birthday, but I also knew I didn't have much of a choice in the matter.

And so what? Life was one big stretch of hurts until your luck turned, until that long golden flip of the coin landed heads up for once. Now, my journey was nearly over. After a whole week of plugging along on that dusty old trail, I was getting close. I had passed through the woods, come into open land. I was in the Riverlands now, where last I heard Pop was living. The hills got hillier and the valleys grew steeper. The road was less crowded, and strange-looking men wandered about, gruff and unshaven. Everything started to smell like fish.

I was headed to Pop's house, and maybe I was the happiest kid in the whole world.

2

IT TOOK A FULL DAY of wandering around and asking, since I didn't exactly know where Pop lived anymore. Every time I'd come across a person I'd ask them if they knew the current residence of David Josiah Pennington, and I rarely got much of a satisfactory response. Either they'd mutter that they'd never heard of the man, or else they'd look scared and hightail it away from me. One plump lady with a toddler crossed herself three times and walked over to the other side of the road as soon as I said his name. Eventually I found a seedy-looking old man tottering around his front yard, his door left wide open.

"Can I help you, sir?" I asked.

"Sure, sure," said the man, swaying a little. "How's about

you draw an old man a cup of water from that well over yonder, how's about it?"

The well was a regular-looking brick thing dug into the man's front yard. That seemed easy enough. When I handed the man the water cup he slurped it all up and motioned for another. It took three before he was satisfied.

He let out a big burp and made to shake my hand.

"Rodney Cleaver," he said. "And who the heck are you?"

"I'm Buddy Pennington," I said. "David Josiah Pennington's son."

The old man squinted and cast a crooked smile at me. "Davey Boy's boy, you say?" I nodded. "Didn't know he had one. Well, that figures, don't it?" The man gestured down the road. "He lives down yonder, about a mile, steady as she goes. Once you get to that big oak tree that looks like it's about to keel over and die, take the trail on your left. Can't miss it."

"Thanks, sir," I said.

The old man just laughed.

Sooner or later I found it.

Turns out Pop was living in an old stilt house hanging over a tiny slough just a short ways off from where it met the river. Pop's house wasn't much, hardly a shack, but right then it seemed the most perfect place in all the world.

Just as the sun set over the cypresses and glinted white

and blinding over the water, I saw him. He sat on a stump outside, his beard scragglier than I remembered it, his clothes a little rattier, sucking on a pipe, black smoke billowing up around him, like he was deep in some sad thought, like he was lost far off in the woods of his brain. He didn't even see me walking up. Never had I thought the day would come when I could sneak up on my daddy.

"Pop?" I said.

He gave a little jump he was so surprised, the pipe snatched back from his lips. For just one second he looked like an animal about to bolt off into the woods and be gone.

But then he grinned, that sly, gold-toothed grin that he said was the key to everything and all of life, the magic to getting whatever you wanted, and his eyes lit up like the bonfires on the levee, and he leapt to his feet and gathered me up and swung me around laughing.

"My boy!" he hollered. "My Buddy boy come all the way down here to see me!"

He set me on the ground and out came the questions, dozens of them, that quick way he has of making you feel like every story you tell is gold, like you're the most important person in the whole world. I told him all about my travels, about the horse with no mane, about the lady kicking me out of her carriage. He about lost his mind laughing over that. He kept calling me "my boy, my boy," and I don't even have to tell you how much that meant to me.

It was just how I'd always dreamed it, just how I'd always wanted it to be.

"So what brings you to my neck of the river?" said Pop, once we sat down in the house, sweet tea for me and a sip out of his jug for him.

"Well, I kinda sorta had to leave Mom's house," I said, "on account of how I lit the oven on fire. But it was an accident, I swear to you." I almost told him about the one-eyed toad, but I didn't much feel like making my dad think I was crazy on our first night back together. So I lied. "I fell asleep, I guess."

"Out all night, causing trouble I bet," he said. "That's my boy. We weren't made for early rising, no sirree. Folks such as you and I, we make our living by night, and the sunrise is just God's way of telling us it's bedtime. You don't learn nothing from a morning anyhow."

"That's right," I said, nodding. "I tried to tell Mom that about a hundred times."

"No doubt you did," said Pop. His face got stern a moment. "You ain't planning to set this place on fire, are you?"

"Nope," I said. "Wouldn't dream on it."

"That's my boy," he said. "Now how about we get us some grub?"

Pop gave me an old pair of his boots, a little too big on me, but they did the job. Then he took me down to a creek where he'd set up some mudbug traps, baited with fish guts and old chicken feet. The traps were full, a massive catch, probably twenty crawling red mudbugs in each. He tossed them still alive in a big black pot and chucked in spices and taters and corn, and when they were good and ready we dumped them out on the table and went to town, cracking the backs and slurping out all the meat and spices, the cuts on my fingers stinging, my tongue like it was about to burn off, all that spicy river food. The best part was sucking the gunk out the head. You couldn't get mudbugs in town, and it had been ages since I'd had them. After we ate, Pop told me stories by the fire, stories of gamblers and bandits and fearsome pirates, all on this river, this very one. He told me about Madame Caravel and how he nearly lost his pinky finger in a knife fight. He told me about getting hexed by a witch lady and how one time he saw the ghost of his old boss Mr. Jim floating over the waters on the exact same spot where he'd drowned.

"What about the Creepy?" I said.

"You mean the baby snatcher?" said Pop. "The one who eats up innocent little children for fun? It ain't true. A fella like that don't exist."

"Well this blind man I met on the road said to watch out for him."

"I lived in these parts my whole life. Don't you think I'd know if there were any baby eaters around? Besides, you come to a legend like that, you always find a person at the bottom of it. An honest-to-God human being. And when it's a human being involved, flesh and blood, same as us, well, ain't nothing too much to be afraid of, is there?" He lit his pipe and took two big puffs. "See Buddy, you can't be trusting any old man you meet on the road. You don't know what such a man wants. You can't trust a person if you don't know their angle. And everybody's got one, of that you can be sure."

"Even Mom?" I said.

Pop laughed. "Don't you doubt one second your mom's got something cooking. That lady schemes more than any person I ever met. Probably why I fell so hard in love with her."

I wanted to ask him another question about Mom, why she had left Pop in the first place. I'd always wanted to know, and every time I asked Mom she'd just go silent, and why would I want to go upsetting my mom like that? So I generally kept mum about the whole thing. But now was my chance. Now I was gonna finally get to know what happened.

"Pop," I said. "I wanted to ask you something."

Pop lit his pipe and leaned back in his old rocking chair. I was sitting on a bait bucket. The whole house smelled like mudbugs and pipe smoke and fish. I was about the happiest a kid could ever be.

"Why'd Mom run off on you like that?" I said. "Why'd she leave the swamp? Why'd you let her take me with her?"

Pop thought a minute.

"Now that's a tough question right there, Buddy," he said. "That might take more time to answer than I got tonight."

"Aw, come on," I said. "You can't say one word about the subject?"

Pop smiled his gold-toothed grin real big and whipped a deck of cards out of his back pocket. He fanned them out wide in his hands.

"Tell you what," he said. "Pick a card, any card. Go ahead now, I won't look."

He shut his eyes and turned his head, all dramatic-like.

I wished Pop would just tell me instead of making me play a game like this. But then again, wishing my daddy was any different than he was was about as useless as wishing the moon would turn purple. All I could do was play along and make the most of it.

I took a good long look at those cards. They weren't normal cards, the kind you play poker with, clubs, spades, hearts, diamonds, all the court folks. No, these were special cards. They were Parsnit cards, the best and most noble game in all the world.

I loved Parsnit cards. They were like playing cards, but they had pictures on them, and you were supposed to tell a story with them. Whoever told the best story won the Parsnit duel. It was a tough game, mind you, and only the best, smartest, cleverest folks ever played it. I remembered Pop and his friends, the whole gang of them, hollering and clapping and telling stories about the wildest duels they played and saw. A true Parsnit duel required the presence of a witch. It was dangerous and mysterious business. You were taking your life in your hands if ever you played Parsnit.

I looked at Pop's Parsnit cards, immaculate and bright in his grubby fisherman's fingers. They didn't have a speck of dirt on them, as if he cleaned them every night, as if there was something magic about them.

"Go on," said Pop, his gold tooth flashing and his eyes shut. "Pick one."

I picked the Fish Boy. He was a sort of short peasant kid who looked normal, wearing normal clothes, and he held a wooden cup in his hands. And popping out of that cup was a great big catfish, glowering at him, whiskers whipping this way and that. The boy looked scared, his eyes all bulging and goggle-like, and all around him people were gasping, their hands at their mouths. All of them recoiling in fright, or else pointing to laugh. It was a scary card, and a sad one. I don't know why I picked it, but I did. There was something about it that felt true to me, like maybe I knew how the Fish Boy felt.

I plucked the card and nearly dropped it. I dunno. It felt as if it was tingling in my hand, like it was moving, like it was alive.

I saw a grin crawl across my daddy's face.

"Very good," he said.

I was nervous, I realized, all sweaty. An owl hooted out-side Pop's window. The weird way the moonlight spilled through the cracks in the walls cast an eyeball-pale glow on the table.

"Now hold that card behind your back," said Pop, "and grip it tight, lest you drop it, lest it gets blown away."

I did it. He snapped the card fans together into one pile, his eyes still shut, his face still turned a little bit away from mine. Then Pop shuffled.

Oh boy, my daddy shuffling cards was a marvelous thing.

The cards flapped in long arcs back and forth, like he was playing an accordion. They flew impossibly high and landed right back down in place, they seemed alive and moving, they danced between his palms like they had a mind of their own, they whirlwinded about his head like any moment they would scatter off and fly away like a flock of birds. But he kept them all under control, he always brought them back together as a deck in his palms. It was mesmerizing, I tell you. I couldn't take my eyes off him.

Pop clapped his hands together like he was praying, then smacked the deck of cards back down on the table. He opened his eyes and peered at me, his grin wide, that gold tooth flashing.

"Is this your card?" he said.

He turned over the top card of the deck. There it was, the Fish Boy.

"But how?" I said. "I got it right here in my hand."

I drew my hand from behind my back.

My palm was empty.

I looked on the floor to see if I had dropped it. I mean, there had to be another one, right? There had to be two Fish Boys. I grabbed the deck out of his hand and flipped through it. Nope, every card was unique, an individual, and there were no duplicates.

"But how'd you do that?" I said. "I had my eyes on you the whole time."

Pop chuckled.

"That, my Buddy boy," he said, "is your problem right there."

"I don't understand," I said.

"You will one day," said my daddy. "Of that I am most confident."

I must've seemed pretty disappointed. Pop spit on his hand and mussed my hair with it. "Don't you worry now. They'll be time enough for all that talk. I sure am glad you came, Buddy. It's about the best gift you could have given me."

That was the kindest thing I'd ever been told. It set all the stars in my heart aglow, hearing Pop say that.

"Now how about we get some shut-eye, eh?" he said.

I realized then how tired I was, from the travel and the food. I couldn't remember ever being so wore out.

Pop slept in a hammock made of old rope that he stretched over the back room of his cabin.

"I'll just take the floor," I said.

"No sirree, you will not," said Pop. There was a small lofted space up above us, by the rafters with heaps of junk on it. Pop stood on a chair and fished another hammock out of the loft and tossed it down to me. "Picked this one up not too long ago. You know, just in case." He winked at me.

We tied the hammock to two beams and made sure it was good and sturdy. Before too long I was up there swinging, amazed at how comfortable I could feel dangling off the ground like that. I listened to the night sounds, the buzz of bugs, the holler and screech of tree frogs, the flitter of bats, the thousand invisible creatures calling out in the night. I had forgotten how loud and sweet river nights could sound. I forgot what a lovely racket all that nature could make.

Out the window I watched the far-off clouds coming dark over the water, the moon a soft pale grandmother wishing us well. I'd be lying if I didn't tell you this was the best night I ever had.

Before long I was sleeping. I only just caught a glimpse of

Pop sneaking out of the shack, a lamp in his hands.

"Where are you going?" I mumbled.

He held one finger up to his lips, met my eyes, and slipped out the door. I fell right back asleep, as if I'd just dreamed the whole thing.

3

I WOKE UP TO A hand clapped over my mouth, Pop's whisper in my ear.

"Get dressed, Buddy, and hurry."

Pop was up already. He had his knife on his belt and a knapsack over his shoulder.

"What are we doing, Pop?"

"Shhh."

I heard the sound of oars slapping the water. Pop's eyes grew wide. He thrust his knapsack into my hands.

"Up in the loft with you!" he said. "Toss that old quilt over you and do not make a peep, promise me? Under no circumstances, not for nothing, unless I tell you otherwise. Got it?"

I nodded, scared as I was, and did what I was told. A million questions fluttered in my head like moths around a candle flame. But I kept quiet.

Pop crouched by the window, a knife clutched at his side. I saw him take a deep breath and stick his head out the window, chancing a look over the waters. The night was calm and moonlit, the hush of the river lapping soft against the shore.

Two arms reached through the window and grabbed Pop by the neck. They yanked him hard into the window frame. His face smacked it. Pop let out a holler and I heard his knife clatter on the floor. A long skinny man dressed in filthy ragged clothes slithered through the window. Pop reached for his knife, and the skinny man kicked it across the room.

The man stood tall and lanky in the moonlight. He had a thick mustache and four glinting earrings in his left ear. His nose was huge and knotty, like it had been busted half a dozen times.

"Thinking of using that there blade against me, your old pal Cecily Bob? You thinking of sticking good ol' Cecily Bob?"

The man kicked my daddy twice, just sucker-kicked him down there on the floor like he was a sack of grain. In the moonglow I saw Pop's nose was all bloody and his lip was busted from where it hit the windowpane.

"Well, well, Cecily Bob, is it? You done worked your way up in the ranks, ain't you boy?" Pop chuckled, spat some blood on the floor. "First time I saw you they wouldn't trust you to carry slop to the hogs without a chaperone."

Cecily Bob grinned. "Wouldn't say what I'm doing now is too different from my old days of slop carrying, would you?"

Pop let out a cackle.

"Touché, Cecily Bob. Still, you'd think Boss Authority would respect me enough to send someone worth a durn."

Cecily Bob whipped a long, chipped knife out of his belt and held it to Pop's throat.

"You best watch your mouth, Davey Boy, seeing as how I got the drop on you so easy," he said, grinning. "Seeing as how you're the one on the floor and I'm the one with the knife."

"Hurry up in there," called a weasely voice from outside. "We ain't getting paid by the hour."

Cecily Bob stuck his head out the window and hollered back, "Hold your horses, a'ight? Patience is a . . . a whatsit?"

"A virtue," hollered the outside voice. "It's a virtue!"

"That wouldn't happen to be my old buddy Mr. Hugo out there, would it?" said Pop.

How did Pop know these guys? Sounded like he hadn't seen them in ages, like they were a part of his life before I was even born. Why were they back now, on the very day I came to see my daddy? What kind of jackpot did he get himself mixed up in?

"Aye," said Cecily Bob. "Me and Mr. Hugo sure did miss you, Davey Boy. It sure is good to have you back."

"Funny," said Pop. "Never thought I'd hear old Mr. Hugo talk virtues."

"And why not?" said Cecily Bob. He bent down over my daddy. "Virtues is what this is all about. Virtues and the payment of debts, I wouldn't doubt it. A person ought to pay his debts now, shouldn't he? Come on now, Davey my boy. A person's got to pay Boss Authority back what he owes him."

Cecily Bob, knife gripped in his teeth, sat on my daddy's back and bound his arms and legs with a rope while Pop didn't hardly say a word. I couldn't understand why Pop lay there and took it.

"I don't reckon my odds are stellar at getting myself out of this predicament, no sir," said Pop. "I don't reckon I got much of a chance at all."

"Now you're speaking truth," said Cecily Bob.

"You're just the best lackey old Boss Authority ever had, ain't you?" said Pop. "You've come a long way for a no-good bootlicker."

Cecily Bob kicked my daddy again. Then he bent down and spoke right in my daddy's ear.

"Maybe I get a little too excited with this here blade and you don't make it there at all, how's about that?" Cecily Bob chuckled and slipped a gag over Pop's mouth. "Now that's much better ain't it? This here's for your protection, Davey my boy. It'll keep you from saying something that might get your throat slit."

I was waiting any moment for Pop to wheel around and choke the man out with his ropes. You think being tied up could stop my daddy? No sir. I was waiting on him to spring to his feet and headbutt the man's teeth in, or maybe wrap him up with his legs and snap his neck. But no, Pop just lay there. I couldn't understand why. Pop wouldn't so much as kick the man in the shins.

That's when I realized it was because of me. Pop was lying there, not fighting back at all, to keep the men from finding me out. I wasn't about to let Pop get kidnapped just because I showed up on the wrong durn day, no sir. I crouched in the loft, about to spring on Cecily Bob. I figured at the least I could bite a hole in his neck, give my daddy time enough to split that sucker in half.

But Pop shot me a look from where he lay on the ground. Our eyes met. His were fierce, and they issued out one single command: *Don't you move, Buddy boy. Remember, you promised. You gave your word.*

My word. That's something Pop held highly, I remembered that, as do all the best hustlers and Parsnit players. A person's only as good as their word.

"You got to pay your debts so's you can always have credit at the table," Pop always said. "A man with no credit is a man with no game. Your word's got to be your bond."

"So what happens when the debt's too high?" I asked him once. "Do you go to jail?"

"Nah, Buddy boy," said Pop. "You're forgetting the very biggest rule of Parsnit there is. You remember it?"

"Yessir." I nodded.

"Tell it to me."

I coughed. "The biggest rule of Parsnit is to make sure there ain't any way for you to lose in the first place."

"That's my boy," he said, mussing my hair.

I wasn't hardly five years old and he was telling me this stuff. It was now so real to me it was like I had it deep under my fingernails. There was no way of getting it out of me. So I kept up in the loft and I made my word my bond and I didn't leap out and wring Cecily Bob's neck.

But durn if it wasn't the hardest thing I ever had to do in my life.

Cecily Bob grabbed Pop like a rolled-up carpet and pushed him headfirst out the window. I heard the sound of a thud, like Pop had smacked on something wooden.

A boat. They were loading him up in a boat, floating right there on the slough.

Cecily Bob slithered back out the window, thunking down on the boat, where I'm guessing Mr. Hugo waited with my daddy. I could hear the both of them laughing, the slap of oars on water.

Now I was faced with a conundrum. On the one hand, Pop told me to stay still. He was quite obviously scared, both for his safety and for mine. These men were killers and they'd bested Pop easy, even if he had let them. What chance did I think I had against them? On the other hand, this was my daddy we were talking about, the man I loved more than any other in the world. Heck, I'd just gotten here, finally met back up with him after years apart, and folks were already stealing him away.

Frankly, that ticked me off. Who were these men to show up and steal Pop away on the very night I came to see him? The nerve of those guys. So what if they were killers? They had my daddy.

I scrambled out of the loft with Pop's knapsack in my hands. I snatched up his knife from the floor and sprinted out the door of the cabin, around back to where Pop kept his skiff. The moon was bright and full, casting a white road down the water. I could see the two men up ahead in a dinghy, rowing fast, my daddy tied up between them.

If I was going to catch them, I had to hurry.

I pushed the skiff into the slough and climbed inside. I paddled my way to deeper water, and before I knew it, the river had caught me.

The current was real strong, I had forgotten that. I had forgotten that even though it looked still and brown and almost solid, like a dirt road, the river was always moving, always churning wild underneath.

"Water," Pop always said, "is the most powerful force on earth."

Mom would snort. She used to be playful back then, when I was a little kid, back in the swamp. I could remember how she'd give Pop a hard time and then giggle when he snapped back at her.

"What, pray tell, is so funny about water being the most powerful force on earth?" Pop would say.

Mom would shake her head. "You're wrong, David. It ain't water that's so powerful. It's love."

Pop would chuckle at that. "Fine, have it your way. Water and love. Nothing's stronger than water and love."

The river was black and the stars shone in it like open mouths. Fog hung low on the water like the river's own breath, and I saw the dinghy, the two men rowing, not too far ahead. I could hear their cackles like goblin laughs, like two little hunched-over demons poking at their prey.

I rowed harder. I let the current yank me, I felt the pull of the river like a strong man reached out to hug me. I saw animals on the riverbank, two deer with black eyes bowing their heads, solemn as angels, and an owl swooped low over us. That could be a good sign, an owl over open water, or a bad one, depending on who it was scrying the omens. Pop always said life isn't so much what happens as who tells the better story about it later.

One way or the other, this would be a heck of a story to tell. Now it was up to me to make sure it had a happy ending, a boy and his pop back together, all the low-down scoundrels vanquished, nothing but glad tidings to sing and happy times to tell about.

Well, here's to all that, I thought, and downriver I rowed.

4

IT WASN'T LONG BEFORE THEY caught wind of me, Cecily Bob and Mr. Hugo. They must have sniffed me out. One after the other their heads popped up to stare at me, and I swear in the moonlight I saw Pop writhing on the floor of the skiff.

I rowed hard as I could, my hands blistered from the oars and my hair damp with sweat. In the moonglow pale spiders scuttled by my feet, stowaways on the skiff's floor. I was gaining on the other boat, somehow I was catching up. I didn't know what I would do when I got there. Something. I had Pop's knife after all, and maybe there was something special in his knapsack I had slung over my shoulder. I sure hoped so. I glanced behind me. I was close enough now I could see the snarl on Cecily Bob's face, his bent and crooked nose. Mr. Hugo's too. He was a squat man shaped not unlike a mole, with a top hat and bug eyes and a little mouth set in an O. I could hear them cursing and swearing at me, I could see the tattoos snaking up Cecily Bob's arms, I remembered the gleaming knife he'd pulled on Pop, chipped and rusty from the blood of all the throats he'd probably sliced and the bellies he'd most likely spilled open.

I realized maybe I hadn't planned any of this too well.

I saw Mr. Hugo fish in his pockets for a minute and pull out a small metal box. I heard him cuss and laugh a little, and I looked back over my shoulder in time to see something spark, and then spark again. He was fiddling with a tinderbox, that's what Mr. Hugo was doing. Only what was he going to light with it?

I saw another sparkle, then the bright white burn of a fuse catching. More cackling, and then the burning thing plopped in the water right next to my boat.

It boomed. Water flew up in the air.

The men on the boat roared with laughter. I bet you could have heard them laughing for miles.

It had nearly got me. Something smelled burnt and I realized the blast had singed my hair. Black powder bombs. Another one fell just in front of the boat. I heard it clunk underwater before exploding just as I passed it. Water splashed me in the face.

They were letting me catch up. They wanted me close as possible so they wouldn't miss. They were going to blow up my skiff.

I tried to slow myself down, but the current was too strong, I was being drug straight for them. I saw Pop kick and struggle in the boat and Cecily Bob whack him with an oar. Mr. Hugo lit another black powder bomb then, held it close to his chest, the fuse burning low. In the starlight I saw his gap-toothed grin.

He was close enough I could hear him giggle.

Then he reared back and hurled the black powder bomb right at my head.

I ducked. It flew just over my noggin, clanking on the floor of the skiff.

The black powder bomb was in the boat with me, fuse burning down to a bare smidgen.

I had two choices.

I could snatch it up and chuck it into the water, pray I was quick enough to keep it from blowing up in my hands.

Or I could abandon ship, fling myself into the river, and hope it would hold me, hope it would carry me on to somewhere safe.

Of course, the bomb blew up before I could make a decision.

The blast flung me into the corner of the skiff, nearly out

of it. I bonked my head something awful, and I looked down and my pant cuff was on fire. I kicked the flames out quick enough, but the worst of all was the hole blown in the floor of the boat. It was about the size of my head I reckon, and black water gushed up through it.

Wasn't any point in bailing the water out. This sucker was sinking, and fast. I gripped tight to Pop's knapsack, still slung over my shoulder, and got ready to say my prayers. That's when I heard Cecily Bob's horrible cackle, and a lit black powder bomb went sailing over my head, the burning fuse streaking across the sky like a dismal shooting star.

It landed with a plop in the waterlogged skiff.

This time it blew me out of the boat. Cinders and wood fell around me like burning rain. I hit the water hard, sinking down, down, my body heavy as a cannonball. Deep beneath the water the river turned and twisted, its undercurrents like a wild mass of tangled hair. Debris snatched at my clothes, twigs and driftwood, sunken boats and storm-thrown trees and old forgotten things. My leg was caught, my pants hooked on something gnarled and twisted. I kicked and I kicked but I couldn't break free. I peered up at the moonlight glimmering on the surface of the water over my head, I imagined the billion stars glittering like all the world's jewels, that perfect beautiful night sky I never was going to see again, there was no chance. I was sure I was going to drown.

I saw what looked like one big eye peer at me and blink,

then dash away. I realized the river was a living thing, full of life and rushing and wild as blood.

Then my foot was free. I don't know how it happened, in that moment I could not tell you. But I kicked and swam hard as I could and my face broke the surface of the water and I gasped in all the air my lungs could handle. I'd never noticed the air before, not really, never thought about what a pure cool breath actually tasted like. Let me tell you, I would never take air for granted again.

A bit of blown-apart boat floated by and I grabbed it, hugged it close to me. It was a huge chunk of the bottom of the boat, big enough for me to crawl my belly up on, so only my feet and arms dangled in the water. With my body on it, the boat scrap stayed afloat, it didn't sink. I could keep my head up, the current dragging me onward, Cecily Bob's dinghy disappearing swift down the starlit river, the two lowlifes who thieved my daddy cackling off into the night.

I worried about gators floating under me long as boats. I worried about their jaws that could crack a man's bones in two. I'd seen them float up before in a body of water so slick and smooth it could have been a footpath, it seemed like the calmest most boring water on earth. And right underneath the surface the whole time is *that*. It's the sort of thing that will make you sit back and take stock of the world and your place in it. It's the kind of thing that makes you scared to set your foot out of doors, if you think about it too hard.

So what I did was try not to think about it at all. I didn't think about gators or snapping turtles or alligator gars, which are like gators on top but with fishtails on their bottoms, sort of like a maniac's idea of a mermaid. I tried not to think of the Creepy either, or fanged fish, which were both supposed to be rumors. I tried not to think of river spirits or dryads or the Dolly Witch or any of the other creatures I'd heard about from my daddy when I was just a kid wandering the Swamplands.

What I did focus on was holding tight to the boat scraps, to keeping the course as long as I could. What if I managed to kick myself all the way over to the bank, against the current, mind you, then what? Hitchhike after the men who stole Pop? They'd be long gone before I could get half a mile. River travel was the only way, and I was now without a boat. It'd take me a miracle, but I was sitting in this river until I wore out or caught them.

At least I had Pop's knapsack. It was soaked on through, probably everything in it all sopping and ruined, but at least I hadn't lost it. There was still that.

I let the river carry me on. There wasn't any other choice in the matter, and that was a fact. I squinted my eyes and set my face firm toward the horizon.

I'm coming, Pop, I whispered to the night. I said it like a prayer, like a promise. *I'm coming to save you.*

5

I FIGURE NOW IS AS good a time as any to try and explain Parsnit to you, since nothing much is happening in this story right now except I'm floating downriver on a blown-up heap of boat all night. I can't promise I'll do a great job or anything, because Parsnit's not an easy game to explain. You have to see it, really, to know what it's all about. You have to be there, to watch the sitting witch pull the magic of the card, to hear the duelers Orating, to feel your hair stand on end when you go along with a story, when you start to believe it yourself.

See, I'm already getting ahead of myself. Here's the basics, as Pop would have me tell it.

Parsnit is a game of chance, sure, but mostly it's a game of storytelling, and of magic. To have a true Parsnit duel, you need two players, each with their own deck, and a witch, who presides over the duel. First, each player shuffles his opponent's deck. All kinds of shenanigans would be possible during this shuffling part of things if there weren't a witch sitting in judgment over the whole affair. If a Parsnit player tampers with another person's cards, well, that witch might just well burn his eyes right out of his skull. Not to mention that Parsnit is a game of honor, and there ain't much more dishonorable than cheating right off the bat.

Next, each player flips over the top card of his own deck until they land on a Person card, like the Fish Boy, or the Rambling Duke or the Dolly Witch. Any Parsnit player worth his salt will flip a Person card—not just any Person card, but the right one for this game, for how he's feeling today, for what his *soul* feels like—in the first flip. If not, it means his deck don't like him anymore. Parsnit decks are finicky, built by magic. They got a mind of their own, is all I'm saying. It won't do to play with an ornery Parsnit deck. They're like a good horse, you know? Won't let a coward so much as sit on them, much less ride. But if the player's worth a durn, and he's got his cards working for him, then he flips his Person card right off.

The player who drew the Person card begins Orating. It's basically storytelling, but it ain't just making things up. It's communicating with the card, it's talking back and forth, saying what you see painted right there in front of you, but also drawing a picture in the minds of everybody listening, so's they can see what you're seeing. You Orate the story well enough and it might as well be real, it might as well be happening right there in that room. This is where the witch comes in. Witches have a way of making the stories pop and sparkle, making them come true as the very air you're breathing. Parsnit ain't Parsnit without a witch in the room. As the Orating goes along, the cards gain their power, they nearly flash and burn with it.

Next each player draws three cards off the top. Again, if they're worth a lick, one of them is gonna be a Home card. Home cards will be where the character's from, or else where the story starts: the Far Yonder Mountains or the Cold Dark City or the Long Lonely Prairie. A setting helps round the character out, it does. You have a person and you have a home, then you got the beginnings of a story.

After the Home cards is when things get trickier. Each Parsnit player draws seven cards, one at a time. These are called the Journey cards, and they're cast one at a time on the other player's character. A Journey card can be anything, really: a place like the Bramble or the Craggly Hills, a different Person card, something trickier too, like Didn't It Rain? or Lilyswamps Bloom or When Your Way Grows Dark. Of course, once a player lays down a Journey card, the other player has to Orate around it. Change the story, adapt, be quick in his mind, make something good. Because you can tell real quick when the Orating goes bad. You get bored, for one. Or worse, the sitting witch gets bored. You'll start sweating, you'll get a burning feeling in your feet. I've heard tell about men gone running straight out the room to dunk their heads in a bucket of water, they were feeling so sick from a round of bad Orating. No bigger shame is there for a Parsnit player.

Once the Journey cards come into play, a Parsnit duel is hard to describe, because there isn't any standard Parsnit duel. Depending on the players and how good they are, a duel could go a million different ways. It could last twenty minutes or two days—who knows? The only rule is you can't take a break, and you can't go to sleep. If the witch can stay awake (and witches have been known to stay awake for weeks if they so desire) then the match carries on, players laying down cards against one another, adapting around them, changing the story. Eventually the two Person cards have to meet. More cards will be drawn, places named, conflicts brought in. Side characters, supporting cards. Heaven help you if a duelist plays a Red Bride against you. Near impossible to beat a Red Bride. She walks right in the room and lays waste to near everything. And if you're not careful, she'll steal the story right from you, and you'll lose. Red Bride's the hardest card to draw, even for an experienced Parsnit player. She bides her own time, only showing up when she best feels like it. As I was saying, Parsnit cards tend to have a mind of their own.

Fine and good, but how do you know when there's a winner?

The answer to that is obvious. How do you know when a story's finished, when it's any good? You just know, is the answer. That, or the player stops Orating and just says, "The end." If he did it right, the whole room will burst into applause. Grown men weeping, women dancing around, clapping their hands like they were in a tent chapel. I've heard of witches themselves shed a bloodred tear for a Parsnit duel well played. If you win, you win, and everyone knows it. Even the cards know it. A losing Parsnit card will sometimes bear a mark, if the shame is too great. Losing in Parsnit is obvious, and the cards themselves feel it too.

Now what exactly is at stake when folks play Parsnit? Well, that depends on the folks playing. Some Parsnit duelists don't play for anything but honor—no wager required, just the thrill of spinning a tale out of skill and chance and magic. Some like to make a little profit here and there, folks like Pop and his old crew, who I knew made most of their living off Parsnit duels. Still others take Parsnit to a more serious level. These folks will wager something permanent, something they can never take back, and seal it with a witch's bond, a sort of burn scar around the ring finger of both duelists. Witch's bonds are forever, unless the witch undoes them, and they can be passed down from father to son, mother to daughter, blood to blood. Many lives have been won and lost in Parsnit, money changed hands, decisions made and decisions forfeited. It's a risky game, that's for sure. And why would anyone risk so much on a card game, on a game of wit and chance and storytelling? What brings folks round time and time again, to talk and jabber, to flip cards and tell their story, to hold real magic in their hands, to watch it flicker and spark across the air and land hot and popping on their tongues? When folks play Parsnit, folks play their dreams.

And that means everything's possible in Parsnit. Everything at all.

6

LATE THAT MORNING I WASHED up in a town
that I figured was Gentlesburg. I don't know why it's called
that, there ain't anything "gentle" about it. Matter of fact, if
what I'd heard about the place was true, I was as likely to
get myself beat up or killed or worse as I was to get a hand-
shake. But I was flat out of food and tired to boot, and
besides, if Cecily Bob and Mr. Hugo had stopped anywhere
along the river before rowing down to the Swamplands,
this would be it. Wasn't any other town after it, not on this
river, not before it became the swamp. Gentlesburg was
right at the border, the meanest, cruddiest place I knew of.
Folks were scared to come here, the boring nice folks from
where my mom lived. They said it was too rough-and-tum-
ble for respectable folks.

Good thing I'm not in the least bit respectable.

I floated past all the big riverboats with all their sails and cargo, early risers loading and unloading boxes and crates and sacks, everything stinking of fish and rotten vegetables and grubby old men, down to a dumpy, rotted pier half-sunk in the water. The only person there was an old woman slumped over in a chair on the dock, snoring. She looked to be about six hundred years old, if you want to know the truth about it.

By then my arms were near numb from holding on to that little plank, and I figured it wouldn't take me another fifty yards, so I hollered up to that sleeping lady.

"Howdy, ma'am!" I yelled. "Little help down here!"

Her eye popped open and she took a gander at me, floating down in the water by the pier.

"You can't dock here, son," she snarled.

"I ain't got any raft," I said. "Just this here plank, and I'm about worn-out from holding on to it."

"How far did you come on that hunk of driftwood?" she said.

"A good night's worth of travel," I said.

"Good gracious," she said, hobbling up out of her chair. "What kind of world is it where children come floating down the river like so much flotsam and jetsam. Durn shame it is, this world. Hateful all around."

The woman leaned herself over the pier and I caught hold

of her hand. She pulled me up all on her own, she did. This woman was awful strong.

"Need a place to sleep?"

I was so tired I nearly keeled over right then, but then I righted myself and shook my head.

"No ma'am," I said.

"I know a rogue when I see one," she said. "Snuck away from my daddy once too, when I was just a kid. He wasn't too nice, not to me or my mom, if you know what I mean. Looking at you, I figure you do."

I was about to correct her but then my stomach growled so big the old lady grimaced.

"Come on then," she said. She led me to a stinking hut with one seaward window just a bit off from the rotted pier.

"My husband built this shack."

"Where's he?" I said.

"Long dead now." She sighed real deep. "Years and years and years."

"So who were you waiting for out there on that pier?"

"Just waiting for my ship to come in, I suppose."

She smiled a little. It was broke-toothed and crooked, and it made me sad. She gave me some bread and cheese and I gobbled them down. My head started nodding a little and I guess she could tell how tired I was, because the old lady pointed to a musty old quilt in the corner of the room. It looked like where a dog might sleep. But that was okay, the way I looked and felt, I'm sure I wasn't much better off than a dog.

I fell right asleep, my daddy's knapsack held tight in my arms.

I woke up, maybe around noonish, because the light shining through the cracks in the ceiling was bright as fire and spears of sunlight glistened all over the floor. The old lady was just sitting there, smiling at me.

"I could've had a boy," she said. "I could've had a son just as you are, if only things had gone different for me."

She was cleaning her fingernails with a knife.

It made me hurt for that lady, and I knew I needed to rise and go find Pop but I was just so tired, so worn-out from floating all night that I could barely keep my head up, I barely could keep awake.

"Came all the way here from a big city up north, with great buildings and churches with stained glass and a bell tower you could hear clanging for miles and miles. I remember what it was like there, the way people spoke, the bright, pretty clothes they wore. I remember so much of where I left. Of course, that's when my Leroy came and swooped me away. Said he heard of a magic game—a card game—folks down toward the Swamplands were playing. Said he had to go there himself to play, that the cards didn't work the further from the Swamplands you moved, that they revolted against the holder, they became nothing but paper. Said if I went down there with him, we'd find our fortune.

"I agreed right away. I didn't hardly know what a swamp was, but I loved old Leroy, and I loved adventure. I wanted to see the world, I did. I wanted to know all that lay beyond the city. I wanted to see mountains and forests, I wanted to float down rivers, I wanted to see the ocean. And I did, I saw all of it, and it was beautiful. And my Leroy was with me through every hill and mountain and river and countryside. Until we came to Gentlesburg, my new home. But then poor Leroy had to go on and get in over his head. Then poor Leroy had to make a wager no one could pay up."

"Why do you stay here?" I said, my voice just a scratchy whisper against all my tiredness. "Why don't you up and leave?"

"Oh honey," she said. "But this is Leroy's pier. He said when he bought it, don't you worry, one day our ship will come in. And old Leroy was a lot of things, but he wasn't a liar. So I'll be here waiting until it does."

The way she sat there, in the shadows, like she was crouching away from the light . . . I don't know, something about it scared me. What loneliness could look like, what it could do to a person. All that time alone, waiting for something that was never going to come. Later I would think maybe I dreamed it, that all this was just a melancholy notion that drifted right into my noggin and swirled around, and through that magic became a dream. I don't know, but I think it was real. I drifted myself right back to sleep.

When I woke up the sky was dark and clear and the moon was bright and wild out the window. I'd slept through the whole durn day. No telling where my daddy was now. The old lady had a plate sat out with some salted fish for me and another scrap of bread. She sat there and watched me, a little grin on her face. I wondered if this was all she had. I wondered what else she would eat.

I sat up and realized something was missing. Pop's knapsack. I must have looked panicked because the old lady said, "Don't you worry now. I just set your things out to dry. Turns out I needn't have bothered."

Laid out on the cabin floor were my daddy's Parsnit cards. That must have been what was in the knapsack, what Pop had entrusted me to keep safe from Mr. Hugo and Cecily Bob. The cards had been floating in water for hours and hours. They should have been soaked through, the colors all run, the cards bent and faded. But nope, they were shining, pristine, same as if they were brand-new.

"Capital deck of cards you got there," she said. "Go on. Ain't a one of them missing, not by my count."

There they all were, and I had them for the first time to myself. I flipped each card over one by one, watched them dazzle in the sunlight. The Corpse Laugher with his dead mouth all twisted and that cackle you could practically hear, the sort of thing that could give a boy nightmares if he dwelt on it too long. The Brightly Shining Dancer with her red cheeks and dark eyes, pigtails coming undone as she twirls. The Lowdown Howler with his pants ripped at the knees, his old mangy hound bawling out the night. I turned over the Plains of Plenty with their rustling fields of golden brown and the Hermit's Woods, a hawk flying black over the treetops. I saw the Far Yonder Mountains and the snow falling calm and quiet over them, a little puff of black smoke coming up from a cabin hidden somewhere deep in those crags.

What was it about these cards that sent a shiver right over me, and had ever since I was just a little kid sitting in Pop's lap? Was it really only a game, something grown folks do for money, or was there more to it than that?

I knew it was hard to get a real good honest-to-God Parsnit deck, though Pop never quite told me the specifics. It wasn't like there was anybody I could ask around our little town after Mom dragged me away from Pop. No, Parsnit was a swamp-folks game, one the townsfolk frowned on if ever they'd even heard of it. Rumor was a witch had to make them for you, a special mix of hexes and conjuration.

Staring at those cards in that old lady's shack brought to mind a memory, like they were speaking the images back to me, straight into my mind.

I wasn't more than four but it came to me in that moment, clear as yesterday. It was an endless winter's night, cold and rainy, fire burning bright, Mom reading a book, Pop with that wild shut-in look glistening his eyes. Pop hated winter, hated being hemmed in by the cold. We'd been sitting like that in peace and quiet all night. It was like Pop couldn't take it anymore. Suddenly he broke the silence of the evening and spoke.

"It takes a great art to make a true deck of Parsnit cards," said Pop.

Pop was sometimes of a mind to make pronouncements like this, and I always waited eagerly for them, especially on boring winter nights like these.

"Yes sir. Try showing up to ol' Baudelaire Quatro's Place with a false Parsnit deck, a pitiful pack of dead paper. They'd right slit your throat for that. They'd tie you to a rock and dump you right in the swamp water."

"Can you teach me to play?" I asked him, for what was probably the ten thousandth time.

Mom looked up from where she sat reading, casting a fierce eye on my daddy.

"Naw Buddy boy," said Pop, chuckling. "You're far too young to be messing around with the sort of riffraff that play Parsnit. Nope, your pop is long retired, he is. Just keep this deck here for sentimental reasons. Like I said, this Parsnit deck here is a work of the rarest of arts."

"The rarest of arts indeed," said Mom, grinning a little.

"It's a fact," said Pop. "This deck here can whoop any Parsnit player in the Swamplands. Provided that the right fella wields them of course."

"Ah yes," said Mom. "The pride of the Parsnit player."

"You saying I should be ashamed of all the duels I've won?" said Pop.

"Oh certainly not," said Mom. "It's just that you have something made by—what'd you call it, the 'rarest of arts'—and all you can think to do with it is make some money."

"It ain't just about the money, and you know that, darlin'," said Pop. "You know good and well Parsnit's about more than that."

"Okay then," said Mom. "It's not just about money. It's also about winning."

That flustered Pop a bit, I could tell. After a minute, Mom lowered her eyes to her book. Pop leaned in close and whispered to me. "Truth is, I'm pretty sure your dear sweet mother would not approve of me teaching you Parsnit. I'd never hear the end of it."

"If you 'dear sweet' me one more time," said Mom, not bothering to look up from her book, "you'll be sleeping in the outhouse tonight."

I must have looked so dejected at that news that Pop said, a bit too loud, "I figure it's okay if I tell the boy the basics, right sugarplum? It sure won't hurt the boy to know a bit about the rules of the game, were someone out there to someday wind up playing it."

Mom sighed a little, but she didn't say anything else.

"I think we're in the clear," whispered Pop. "Okay, here's the basics. Parsnit tells a story, each card does, the chance of it, the cunning of the player, how well he can react. How well he knows his cards, and how well his cards know him."

"How can cards know a person?" I said.

"That's one of the great mysteries of the game, ain't it? And oh what a powerful sight it is to see two Parsnit masters at play. You watch how the two dueling stories become one, how they turn and tangle into the same story, how they set off on a journey together, where only one player can come out alive. It's downright intoxicating, it is, both for the players and for the crowd. And I imagine for the cards as well."

Pop had this far-off sparkle in his eyes, and I knew it wasn't any good interrupting him now, that even if I asked for an explanation it would be so long-winded and glassy-eyed I couldn't make much sense of it. But then I thought of another question, one more practical, and I couldn't help but ask it.

"Pop," I said, "have you ever lost a Parsnit duel?"

Pop looked down at the table a minute and popped his knuckles.

"Never have," he said. "And I can tell you right now that I never will." He slapped the table. "You know what? I don't think your mom will mind if we have a little fun here, will she?"

Mom didn't move. She just kept reading, or at least acting like she was. But she wasn't turning the pages anymore.

"Fine, fine," said Pop. "Watch this."

He picked up the Parsnit deck and began to shuffle the cards, which was always a sight. They were flying every which way like sparks shooting off his fingers, all landing like magic right back in Pop's hands. You never seen cards fly so fast as when Pop shuffled a deck. You were afraid to stick your hand out lest the cards be moving too fast and you wind up losing a finger.

"Tell me when to stop," said Pop.

"When!" I said.

Pop scooped all the cards together and slapped them down on the table, a tall flat deck, perfectly uniform, sitting there like a gold brick.

"Now put your hand on it right there, Buddy boy," he said. "Touch the deck lightly, with just your fingertips."

I did what Pop said.

"Clear your mind now. Make it absolutely blank and empty, like the night sky without any moon. Can you do that? Sure you can, sure you can. Now when your mind is absolutely clear, I want you to listen. Listen with your fingers now. What are the cards saying to you? What do they whisper?"

I couldn't hear a word. I mean it. Not one tiny sound. Just maybe a little snicker coming from Mom in the corner.

"Now flip over the first card," said Pop.

I did.

"What do you see?"

I did it now too, in this very moment, in the old lady's shack. I flipped over the exact same card I had in my memory: the Fish Boy. There he was, looking all baffled and confused, that fish poking right out of the cup of water like it was wanting to whisper him a secret.

But tonight the Fish Boy had changed. A softening of his eyes. They had gone brown, a little green to them. His face wasn't so round and red this time. No, it was skinny and pale, his chin sharp now, his eyebrows furrowed like he was wondering about something.

Yep, the Fish Boy looked like me.

I mean just like me. We could have been twin brothers. We could have been the exact same person.

Had he always looked like me? Or had something changed?

There was something to these cards all right, and it spooked me good. I peered close at that card. It was like the Fish Boy was looking straight at me. I thought I saw the card smile.

The old lady coughed. I snapped right out of my daydreaming.

"Like I said," croaked the old lady, "capital deck of cards you got there."

Enough of that. I wrapped the cards back up in their cloth and put them in the coffin box and hid them in the knapsack.

I promised myself one day I would come back and help her out if I could, same as she helped me. I promised myself that, even if I was a scoundrel and worldly and all that, the least I could do was help this old lady out. I swore it, right then and there.

"Thank you, ma'am," I said. "I can't thank you enough."

"If you're searching for somebody, you'll head to the Skinny Yellow Dog, you will," she said. "Tavern down about that way. If a fella's anywhere, he'll be there."

"Thank you again, ma'am," I said.

"It's no trouble in the world," she said. "Not like any trouble I already seen. I been lost before and nobody helped me. I been all alone and stayed that way."

I gripped my daddy's knapsack close to me and turned to go.

"Sonny?"

"Yes, ma'am?"

"If I were you, I'd be mighty careful about who I let see those cards of yours," she said.

"Thank you, ma'am," I said. "I'll guard them with my life."

"Hope it won't come to that," said the old lady.

For a second I thought she was kidding, but the lady didn't smile any. That didn't make me much feel good, if you want me to be honest about it.

7

I WALKED DOWN THE DIRTY dusty streets. Men hung on street corners smoking and scowling, and women stood around in groups, laughing meanly.

"You know where the Skinny Yellow Dog is?" I asked an old man with buckteeth.

He just sneezed on me.

I tried a young lady, maybe twenty-two, tall and pretty with a long flowy dress.

"Skinny Yellow Dog?" I said.

"Three blocks thataway," she said, gesturing with a white-gloved hand, "and take a left."

"Much obliged," I said, and gave her a bow.

"What a little gentleman you are!" She giggled at me,

which made me feel ridiculous. "What are you looking for a place like that for?"

"I'm trying to find the two low-down varmints who kidnapped my daddy."

"Gracious lord alive!" she said. "You're a cute one, you are. And your daddy got kidnapped? My, my." She leaned in close to me. "Revenge is a tricky business. Perhaps I could interest you in one of these?"

She opened her petticoat to reveal a whole arsenal of knives sewn into the lining. The pretty woman slipped one out, a nasty little thing.

"You can really stick somebody good with this one. But you gotta be quick. Once in the belly"—she poked me a little, not too hard, but enough to give me shivers—"then once slow across the throat." She drew a cold line soft across my Adam's apple. "Could be yours, just cost you a bit of silver is all."

I stammered, backing away from her. She stood there, a big smile on her face, that knife cold and gleaming.

"No thank you, ma'am," I said. "You be having a good evening though."

"It isn't safe," she said. "Walking into a place like the Skinny Yellow Dog without any protection."

"I'll be careful," I called to her, still backing away.

"Sorry is what you'll be!" she hollered, and gave me a

dainty little wave. "Toodleloo!"

Well, so far I'd been heckled, sneezed on, and offered weaponry. I guess Gentlesburg was every bit as wicked and low-down as folks said it was. I had a thrill just walking down the street, seeing people leer at me from under caps and through grubby windows, wondering at me just like I was wondering at them. It made me feel like a baby mouse scuttling through a whole yard full of snakes, each one sizing me up. Maybe I should have bought a knife from that lady. Maybe I should have had some money on me. Maybe I was in way over my head here, chasing down the two killers who made off with my daddy.

I looked up at the moon and stars, I heard the river lap up against the pier, I felt the knapsack full of my daddy's Parsnit cards.

I needed to get my mind right.

Pop always said, "You win at first sight. An ace hustler wins just by walking into the room, if only your walk is good enough."

I wasn't any mouse running scared through a yard of snakes. I was the durn snake. And all those creepy no-goods gaping at me with their peepers better remember it. And I strutted all the way to the Skinny Yellow Dog.

I found it, three stories tall and at a weird angle, like it was about to topple over into the street. The windows were lit bright and the doors were wide open and it seemed stuffed full of people, like any moment arms and legs would start dangling out the windows because there wasn't space inside for them anymore. I could hear music and laughing and cussing and hollering, cigar smoke lingering around like a fog of lazy ghosts.

It seemed like just the place for a kid like me.

I walked my swaggering self right through the front doors, and nobody even said a word to me about it.

It was even wilder inside.

There were scraggly fellows with big bushy beards and folks with scars all over their faces and women with rings on their ears and lips and noses who scowled and spit and roared louder than the men. A woman with long black hair and a red hat played the fiddle while a man stomped and hollered and strummed a guitar. A one-eyed man danced on a table, banging a spoon into a metal plate. Barefoot women turned circles, their dresses floating out like jellyfish. Another fella walked around on his hands, a knife carried between his teeth. Best of all was a pale boy about my own age, wearing a tuxedo and a top hat. The pale boy was a magician. He grinned and pulled a large-mouth bass out of his top hat. The bass was alive and wriggling in his hands. The pale boy bowed while folks threw coins at his feet. I wanted to clap for him myself. I never saw a fella pull a fish out of a hat before.

Food and drink and card games were going all over the

place, every table filled with chattering, screaming, dancing people. The smell was tremendous. There were folks from all over, folks from lands I'd never even heard of, a million different accents and faces and ways of being, each one more fascinating and beautiful than the last. Never in my dreams had I imagined a place so fearful and noisome as the Skinny Yellow Dog. It was wonderful. I felt like Heaven was a gutter and I'd just stepped right in it.

"Excuse me, ladies and gentlemen," I said.

Nobody listened.

"I need to find passage to the Swamplands."

Nothing.

"Some bad folks stole my daddy and I need help."

You couldn't hardly hear me over the fiddle and the dancing and the knives scraping plates.

"This is durn useless."

I saw a girl dressed in rags begging. She was going table to table, holding out a tin cup, clinking the change in it. People ignored her or yelled at her or told her to bug off. She seemed so tired and sad and innocent. It made me mad the way folks were treating her. It made me mad I didn't have anything to give her myself.

"Please, sir," she said to one bearded man. "I just need some food for me and my granddad. We're starving, we are. We're plum out."

"Scram, you little cockroach," said the man, and shoved the girl down. Her change went sailing across the floor.

I took a step toward her, like I was going to jump in and do something about the man, or at the very least help her gather her coins back.

Then I took a look closer. The girl straggled to her feet, all limping-like, her face hidden from the bearded man by her hood. But from my angle I could see that she had a wad of bills in her left palm and she was smiling something secret. That's when I realized it.

The girl was a pickpocket. She wasn't begging, she was distracting folks while she robbed them blind.

She caught me looking at her and winked.

I don't know. That showed some spunk. You got to admire a person like that.

Something about her made me brave. So I cupped my hands and shouted as loud as I possibly could.

"Excuse me, everyone! I am looking for my pop! His name is David Josiah Pennington and he was kidnapped by two low-down scoundrels and that grizzled dog Boss Authority!"

A hand clapped over my mouth. I was yanked backward and tumbled over something stuck out, like a foot.

"What are you doing, you idiot?" said a girl's voice. "Looking to get yourself killed?"

I tried to mumble back but her hand was strong and she

had my arm twisted behind my back. It hurt. This girl had some strength to her.

"You better hope nobody else heard you, boy," she said.

That made me scared a little bit. I looked around the room, trying to see if anybody was noticing us. The music was loud and wild, and people were munching fried catfish and fried chicken and sopping up gravy with cornbread and slamming frothy mugs onto tables, same as before. The pale magician cocked an eye at me, but then he turned his head back to his magic hat. I was pretty sure no one even noticed I was there.

"If I let your arm go, will you promise not to say another word about Boss Authority?" she said.

I nodded.

"Okay, I'm trusting you."

She let go and I whirled around. It was the pickpocket girl. She had deep brown skin and green eyes. She grinned at me.

"My name's Talia, but everybody calls me Tally. What's yours?"

"None of your business," I said. I was all huffy. How was I going to find my daddy now?

"It isn't, is it?" she said, her hands on her hips, like she was bossing me. "Well, you just about told the whole tavern your business. How your daddy is the notorious Parsnit hustler

David Josiah Pennington—"

"That's my pop!" I said, all proud.

"—and now they're all thinking about how they can kidnap you and get a leg up at the Parsnit table, weasel your pop with a witch's bond."

I didn't much like the sound of that, not at all, but Tally was just getting warmed up.

"And on top of that, you were ludicrous enough to say"— she dropped to a whisper for this next part—"Boss Authority is after your daddy? Here? Not a soul in here don't hate Boss Authority, plain as day. Twisted, he is, gone deep rotten with borrowed magic. And yet not a soul in here wouldn't split a belly to be on his good side. You know that old saying, 'the swamp's always creeping'?"

"Yeah, I know it," I said. "It means that the swamp is always moving a little upriver, inch by inch, and one day it'll take over the whole world. It's what folks say when they mean for you to stay ready and vigilant."

"Exactly," said Tally. "And it's the same way with Boss Authority. He's always gathering his magic, killing people and worse, all to gain more power. Pretty soon he'll rule the whole swamp. And as the swamp creeps upriver, so will Boss Authority's rule. Let's face it, if Boss Authority's after your daddy, he's probably after you too. So I figure at this point, half the tavern wants to kill you for who your daddy is, and the other half is just ornery and wants to kidnap you and bring you to Boss Authority as a favor. If I were you, I'd come with me. I can take you to my granddad. If anybody knows where your daddy is, it'll be him."

I studied her a minute. Maybe her granddad knew something and maybe he didn't. Maybe the whole thing was one big setup and I was about to stumble myself right into it. I'd gotten lucky—a rare thing for me, mind you—finding that old lady at the dock, even if she did scare me a little. Did I dare push my luck further with some other old fogey? Besides, what did I know about this girl in front of me? Well, she was a pickpocket, and she might have saved my life. At the same time, she might also be lying to me. She might have just kept me from finding my daddy. All the while, time was a-wasting, Pop getting further and further on down that river without me.

"No thanks," I said. "I had about enough of strange old folks today, if that's all right with you."

Just then I noticed a pigeon perched on a beam about level with my head. The whole place was rotten with pigeons, cooing around on the floor with their funny head-bobbing walk, kind of pretty birds but kind of like rats too. I never did quite know what to think about pigeons, if you want to know the truth about it. But this one was different. For one, it was staring right at me. I mean that. Its head cocked a little to the side, but its gaze fixed on me, like it was waiting on me to up and talk to it.

Also the thing had one eye, a big one, right there on its forehead, boring right into me. It was just like that toad I'd seen the day Mom's bakery burned down, the one that had mesmerized me. The one that had . . .

"Nice Parsnit deck," said Tally. "How'd you get it? Huh? Did you steal it?"

Somehow she'd slipped Pop's Parsnit deck right out of the knapsack and I hadn't even noticed. Tally sure was one heck of a pickpocket. I tried to snatch it back, but she yanked it away again. By God, she was quick.

"Where'd you get it from, boy?" she said. "I happen to know a lot about Parsnit, and I know this ain't yours."

"Just give it back to me, okay?" I said.

"At least tell me your name," she said, "so I don't have to keep calling you 'boy' like a durn idiot."

"Fine," I said. "My name is Buddy."

"Pleasure to meet you, Buddy," she said. Tally smiled at me like she meant it. Still, I didn't like getting pickpocketed, even if it was by a nice person.

"Just give me my daddy's cards back," I said.

Her eyes grew wide. "This is Davey Boy Pennington's Parsnit deck? The famous one that . . . Hey, wait a minute. Why doesn't he have it on him? Every Parsnit player always carries his deck around with him. They get all twitchy when you separate them. I've seen it a million times."

"I told you already, he got kidnapped. Now can I have it back or what?"

"Sure," she said, and held the cards out to me. I snatched them back and tucked them away in the knapsack. I was going to have to keep a much better lookout on my stuff henceforth if I was going to make it out of Gentlesburg in one piece. "I really think you should come see my granddad *right now.*"

"I told you I ain't got time for your granddad," I said. "I'm not trying to be rude, really I'm not, but I got to find Pop." Then something occurred to me. "Hey, did you happen to see a one-eyed pigeon?"

"A what?"

"Never mind," I said. "It ain't important."

I turned to go, make my way around the Skinny Yellow Dog, see if I couldn't rustle up some answers for myself.

"You know," said Tally, "I can show you a Parsnit duel."

That stopped me cold. A real live Parsnit duel? One I could watch with my own eyes? It had been so long since I'd seen a real Parsnit duel, with a witch and everything.

"Yep," she said, like she could read my thoughts. "A good one too, with real Parsnit players, not like those jokers upriver. They hold them in a secret room in the basement. I'll take you there, no problem. The men who kidnapped your daddy are probably there right now."

She did have a point. I mean, where else would I find Pop

if not around a Parsnit table somewhere? It was as good a shot as any.

"Fine," I said. "Let's go."

Tally smiled at me. I don't know, that made me feel good, to be honest with you. I was wondering if finally I had made a friend.

8

TALLY LED ME DOWN A staircase, musty and winding, through a kitchen filled with steam and fire and pots and pans. A skinny man tossed vegetables up in the air, shouting, while a big lady chopped fish heads and screamed back at him. I stopped to stare a minute as she conked a still-wriggling catfish on the noggin, sliced its head clean off, and chucked it at the man. He caught it in one meaty fist, fish guts exploding all over his apron. The man began to shout while the woman cackled and tossed her knife in the air. It stuck right into the ceiling.

"Hurry!" said Tally. "You don't want to be there when they really get into it."

She led me through a trapdoor, up a weird scaffolding,

onto the rafters in the ceiling, through a hole in the wall, to a beam overlooking a tiny, lamplit room, where two sweaty men sat at a table, cards out in front of them. A straight-backed beautiful woman elegantly dressed who I took to be a witch sat hovering just a tiny bit over her chair, like her body never quite touched the furniture. The duel was still in the early stages, the men having just flipped their top cards over until they landed on a Person card. Pop always said if you knew your deck, really truly knew it same as you do your own left arm and fingers, then you could summon the card you wanted, that you could draw it out of the deck first every time, no matter who shuffled.

"But Pop," I had said, "that's like magic."

Pop just nodded. "Sounds about right to me."

At one end of the table sat a man with a long mustache, twisty and droopy that dangled far off his face like catfish whiskers and dribbled down to his chin, with a great big sun-faded cowboy hat on his head. He was skinny and dusty-looking, like he'd been riding around on his horse all day. He took huge glugs from an unmarked jug next to him every minute or so. He had drawn the High Lonesome Traveler, with his fiddle and horse and clouds of dust behind him, that haughty chestnut horse swaggering through the desert like all that hot and lonely didn't bother him one bit. The other player was a black lawyer-looking fella with a nice suit and a monocle. He chewed a cigar but wouldn't light it. He had drawn the Ornery Banker, and you could tell he was mighty excited about it.

The players turned their Home cards next. The lawyer flipped a Cold Dark City and smiled a little. This was a man who knew his cards all right.

The lawyer began to Orate.

Now, this is the part where Parsnit gets tricky. It's hard to explain just what happens when a player begins to Orate. It's something to do with the cards, how the cards are specifically theirs, how well they know their cards, each tiny detail of them, and how well the player can tell the cards' story. Because Parsnit is all about storytelling, when you get down to it. It's about weaving a story with the cards, until the two players weave their stories into one.

Orating is the best part of the whole game. I had a feeling about this lawyer fella. He was about to do something incredible, that I knew.

The lawyer's voice was strange-accented, like it had picked up a little bit of here and there along the way. It was rich and gentle, a good dessert of a voice, like hot cider on a cold night. And that's what I felt all of a sudden, with a chill— I was cold. The Parsnit cards were working, the lawyer was telling the right story for them. I heard him tell of a man gone a long way off for business—his person, the Ornery Banker, the card that always irked me, because who would want to be an Ornery Banker when you could be a Rambling Duke or a High Lonesome Traveler or even a Fish Boy? But as he Orated I began to feel for the person, just a little bit. I was cold and wet and my legs hurt from tramping through the snow, and I ached in my bones for home.

See, all Parsnit decks are a little bit different, that's a fact, though they all are based on the same ideas, the same places and people and pictures. The difference is in the details. Like Pop's Cold Dark City card was the absolute pits. The snow comes down long and heavy in great gray streaks, and a woman drags a screaming kid through muddy streets, and the kid has lost his shoe, you can see it sticking up in the mud, all the snow half-melted and sludgy and black. Pop's Cold Dark City card was the worst and most miserable place I could imagine folks living.

But the lawyer's Cold Dark City was a different place entirely. Yeah, the snow was coming down thick and heavy, and the town seemed grim with darkness. But that wasn't all. The snow was piled in soft white clouds all over the rooftops, like something you could fall down in and it wouldn't hurt. The mom and child darted through the streets, same as Pop's, only the kid didn't have his boot stuck, and there was someone waiting for them—the daddy maybe—on the front porch, his hat in his hand, the door wide open. They were heading home. This was the story the lawyer was Orating, this was the exact perfect story his cards wanted him to tell.

I began to see the scene with my own eyes, the card wafting through my brain, the ice and snow, that poor man having made it back from his long journey in time to welcome his wife and kid home from church. Just listening to him you could imagine hot coffee waiting for you, a warm fire and thick blankets and maybe even a dog, yapping and running around and licking all the melting snow off your hands. It was a happy home in the Cold Dark City, that's for sure. When he finished Orating the snow on the card seemed to twinkle and flurry, and I saw the lawyer's mouth twitch, just a little hint of a smile. He had given the card power, or else the card had called that power out of him. Only the sitting witch knew for sure.

The scene faded before me, and even the witch had gone misty-eyed. That's how you do it. It was going to be tough for the cowboy to top that one, I knew it.

The cowboy was sweating, oh man was he. He took a big long glug from his jug and spat once on the floor, doing a little shimmy from his boots to his hat. He coughed and flipped his next card.

It was the Far Yonder Mountains, and you could tell it was not the card he wanted, not one bit. The cowboy banged the table and cussed. The witch sat stock-still, floating a bit over her cushion. The lawyer leaned back in his seat and chewed his stogie like he didn't have a care in the world.

A Parnsit duel can surprise you, it really can. You never

know what a player's got up his sleeve. You never know what bewilderment can spring from some little well-dressed nobody's voice.

I couldn't wait to hear the cowboy try and Orate himself out of this one.

Man, I was just so happy to be sitting here, watching a real live Parsnit duel. It had been ages and ages. I shifted on the rafters and they made a little noise but no one noticed. I turned to say something to Tally, like good gracious wasn't this just the most exciting Parsnit duel ever?

When I realized she wasn't next to me anymore.

I patted Pop's knapsack and found it open, and empty. She had thieved me, right there, while I was watching the Parsnit duel. She had Pop's cards.

I just caught a glimpse of her scurrying across the beams, to the hole in the wall, her brown ragged cloak vanishing into the darkness.

If I didn't hurry I was going to lose those cards for good.

I scooted myself across the rafters and crawled through the hole and headed back into the tavern. My balance was a little shifty, and twice I almost reeled. But I had to find Tally. I had to get my daddy's cards back.

I hustled through the kitchen, past the lady who was chucking fish heads at the screaming cook, through the Skinny Yellow Dog as heads turned to watch me go, but I couldn't worry about that, I couldn't. I caught a glimpse of

Tally's brown cloak wisping down an alley, so I followed it.

I sprinted so hard I got a stitch in my side. I scrambled through the streets, bumping into strangers, knocking a cigar from a mustached man's lips. It fell, scattering little gold nuggets across the pavement, while the man stood shaking his fist at me. "Sorry!" I yelled, but I kept moving, I had to.

I saw Tally pause a moment and glance back at me, her eyes catching mine, that little thief, and she took off running again. Why had she stopped to look back, like she was trying to make sure I was keeping up? I had no choice but to follow her down an empty alley. I hopped a stray cat lazing belly down in the dirt. Tally hit the end of the alley and flung open a door I could hardly even tell was there. It led to a staircase, and she launched herself up, and I followed her, you bet I did, I wasn't letting her get away with my Pop's Parsnit cards, not on your life. They were Pop's livelihood, his prize possession, and he entrusted them to me. He wasn't gonna let any Cecily Bob or Mr. Hugo have them, and I wasn't going to let any two-bit pickpocket have them neither, not even if she was a nice pickpocket, one who saved my life once already.

The stairs twisted and turned and spiraled, blind corner after blind corner, each one a perfect hiding spot for someone who wanted to murder me. The stairs led to a hallway with doors on each side, and I saw Tally dart through one of them. I was coming, slow, sure, but steady, I was coming for her, I was coming to get my daddy's cards back, yes sir.

I turned that corner and lunged through that doorway and there she stood, Tally the Pickpocket, in a tiny room stuffed high with books and glass vials and bundles of sticks and stones and jars of herbs and a bird or two flitting around their cages. The birds were lemon yellow and bright shining, like God had taken a sunbeam and shaped it right into an animal.

A tall skinny old man with a fringe of bushy hair and big bug-eyed spectacles sat in a chair in front of me.

"Buddy, this is my granddad," said Tally. She held the Parsnit deck out to me like it was a present. I took it back, warily, like there was some kind of catch.

"I don't get it," I said. "Why'd you steal the cards if you were gonna just give them right back to me?"

"How else was I supposed to get you to Granddad's?" she said, shrugging. "I told you he'd know where your daddy was, if anybody did. Heck, if I'd have let you wander around the Skinny Yellow Dog asking after Boss Authority all night, you'd be hogtied in the back of some river bandit's skiff, headed into the swamp right now."

Well, she had me there.

"Besides," said Tally, grinning, "when was the last time you had a good meal?"

"Some old lady gave me some salt fish a couple of hours ago."

"Let me tell you, Buddy boy," said Granddad, "my stew is a heck of a lot better than some cold old salt fish, and you can swear on it." His voice was high and rickety, like an old warped board someone just stepped on. I kind of liked it, to be honest. I liked his stooped back and suspenders and well-darned slacks. He looked like a gentleman inventor, he did, like somebody always sussing out the secrets of the universe. Hard not to like a fella like that.

Granddad reached his hand out to me, and I took it, because Pop always said you never refuse a hand when it's offered out to shake.

"Charmed," said Granddad.

His hand was long and thin, his fingers spidery and strong. He had a grip like a durn bear trap, and his eyes gleamed with a little silver light.

"Told you you'd like my granddad," said Tally, and she was right.

Granddad set the table and ladled out the soup. When he stood to his full height, I realized just how tall Granddad was—near seven feet probably, and he was skinny as a pike pole. He put you in mind of a bug, like a praying mantis, or maybe one of those suckers that never move and just look like sticks. What do you call those? Stick bugs. Harmless things, stick bugs, and I always kind of liked them.

We all sat down at the table together, in the warm comfortable kitchen, like a real family does. It was nice, I tell you.

It was the most at-home I'd felt in ages.

And the soup was good, too. Potatoes and okra and green beans, some catfish bits floating in there. A real muck of a stew, and spicy to boot. Granddad offered me a second bowl, and I was not too proud to take it. Hunting down your kidnapped daddy is an awful lot of work, it is.

"Now Buddy," said Granddad, after I'd finished eating and Tally cleared the table. He leaned in close to me, his breath tangy with fish and chili pepper. "Tally tells me you're looking for your pop, is that right?"

"Yes sir," I said. "David Josiah Pennington, you ever heard of him?"

Granddad nodded his head. "I do believe I've heard the name."

"Doesn't surprise me much," I said. "Seems like everybody around here's heard of my pop, and only about half of them like him much."

Granddad peered at me, his eyes wide and silvering under those glasses. "I haven't heard anything about your father in quite a while, to be honest. But I have some associates in town, some eyes and ears around. I could ask them for you, if you'd like?"

"Oh yes, sir," I said. "I sure would appreciate it."

"Gonna have a pip on my pipe first," he said, "if that's all right with you." He reached a long skinny arm up to the top of his bookshelf and pulled down a curved wooden pipe, along with a little leather pouch of tobacco. "Helps with digestion, you understand?"

Frankly, that kind of annoyed me a bit. I wanted to find out about my daddy now, not after the old codger had a smoke. But he was doing me a favor, wasn't he? It wouldn't do to complain about a favor. Nope, I'd just have to be patient.

"And that was your daddy's Parsnit deck my granddaughter was holding?"

"Yes sir," I said. "That's how Tally got me up here. She stole it from me."

I winked at her, but she didn't smile back.

"That Tally," he said, laughing. "She's a pistol, ain't she? A real spitfire, she is. Don't know what I'd do without her."

"She's pretty talented, that's for sure," I said. "Never saw a thief work like she does. No offense."

Tally just stared back at me all weird and quiet. I wondered what was ailing her.

"None taken," he said. "It's hard out there these days, with Boss Authority ruling the swamps, always threatening to move upriver. Hard indeed to make an honest living. Now can I see those cards?"

"Pop's cards?"

"Yes sir," he said, puffing his pipe. "It sure would be something special to see old Davey Boy's famous deck."

"Well, all right," I said, looking over at Tally. She was just sitting there frowning at me.

I spread the cards out on the kitchen table as best as I could. I'm normally real particular about showing Pop's deck around—especially after the old lady on the pier's warning—but Tally was awful nice and Granddad just fed me the best meal I'd had since I left Pop's house and well, I was feeling pretty good about things at that moment. I mean, I'd just seen part of a real Parsnit duel, with real expert Parsnit players. I still felt a tingle in my throat from it, a spark in my fingers and toes, like if I touched a doorknob I'd shock myself. I guessed magic left a residue, especially the magic of Parsnit. I could see why folks played the game night and day. I could see why they always wanted a little more. It had grown dark in the room, and Granddad lit a lantern.

Pop's cards sparkled in the lantern light. I was beginning to see the stories in the cards, the way the pictures whispered their tales to me, they seemed to glisten with their own secret life. I wanted to stare at those cards for hours, to hold them and whisper to them and hear them whisper back, I wanted to know their stories and for them to know mine. I wanted to disappear inside of them, wander around for a while and see what I found. I wanted to walk the Staggerly Road, nothing but a jug and a mangy dog at my side. I wanted the company of the Dolly Witch, to let her scatter her bones and tell my stories and see what the starshine showed in her scrying crystal. I wanted to nap in the Bramble with a fox at my side, protected deep in the warm grass, surrounded by a tangle of thorny vines. I wanted to watch the Skeleton Dance, the skeletons all tucked away behind a tombstone as they mocked death and the end, how you could never tell if they were smiling or if that was just their faces. It was true that the skeletons in the Skeleton Dance were supposed to be exactly alike, but that wasn't the case, not when I peered close. Some were taller and some shorter and some had bigger skulls and longer arms. We were all still different in death, I decided. Life never really ended.

I shook myself awake then, wondered how long I'd been staring so deep into those cards. Across from me Granddad smiled, like he knew. His long fingernails scraped the surface of the cards, tracing all the mysteries hidden with them.

"Quality deck of cards, yes sir," said Granddad. "Made by the finest hand, sewn by deep magic."

"Magic?" I said.

"Surely my boy you know how a Parnsit deck is made."

"Well, not exactly," I admitted. "I do know a witch has to make them, but I don't know how."

"There ain't any one way of course," said Granddad. "Every witch has their own particular Parsnit brew, that's a fact. Some use fungus and cat's fur to conjure the pictures. Some mix sticks and twigs and a saint's pinky finger and watch the images appear. Every witch puts a little of herself—a little of her soul—into a Parsnit deck. That's why they're so rare, and so valuable."

Tally sat slumped in the corner, a big old frown on her face. What was the matter with her?

Granddad cracked his long knuckles, and it gave me shivers.

"There is one thing, however, that all Parsnit decks do require. You know what that is, boy?"

"No sir," I said.

Granddad's pipe had gone out, and he laid it now on the kitchen table.

I was feeling the creepers just about then, like something was sneaking up on me. I looked around the room. It was nothing but shadows and old junk. Tally's sad little pallet on the floor, Granddad's musty tangled bedsheets. What was I so worried about just now? A spider scuttled across the floor by my boot. It was a big sucker and I wanted to stomp it, but I found I couldn't, not in a million years. My leg frankly did not want to lift.

"Blood," said Granddad.

"Blood?" I said.

"Not just any blood," said Granddad. "Lucky blood. The blood of the luckiest fella one can find. No good higher priced than lucky blood, no sir. Some witches, they use a drop or two. Others find lucky blood is more potent by the gallon."

"Tally, what's going on here?" I said, but she wouldn't

answer me. She turned around in her chair and faced the corner, like she was being punished, like it was too much for her to watch.

Granddad lifted his sleeve and a spider crawled out, to the tip of his long bony finger. Then it spun a web, dangling down like a puppet string, spinning right before me, in front of my eyes.

It was a dark brown skinny thing, its six eyes flashing their blackness at me, like the opposite of stars, a hole that could suck you clean in. It clicked its fangs and I was mesmerized. I could not avert my eyes, I could not lift my arms to protect myself. I was stuck stock-still. Not even my toes could wiggle.

"Tally?" I said again, my lips barely moving.

"I'm sorry, Buddy," she said. "I really am."

"Your daddy is David Josiah Pennington, eh?" said Granddad. "I wasn't sure till I saw the deck, but oh yes, it's his all right. Davey Boy Pennington, the man with the luckiest blood in sixteen counties. A man infamous for crossing the right folks and befriending all the wrong ones. The man who won and lost more fortunes than could ever be counted. The biggest, luckiest scoundrel that ever crawled the river."

Granddad rose from his chair. His arms stretched out wide and long and skinny like tree limbs, they seemed to grow. He set his glasses on the table. His eyes seemed to change now, to become darker, black almost. He leered down in my face and smacked his lips. I said he looked like a stick bug, but no, that wasn't right. Those long skinny arms, those well-black eyes. Naw, he was something closer to a long spindly spider, that's what he was, same as the spider dangling from his finger.

"You're his son ain't you?" he said. "Then you got his heart, you do. Scoundrel you are, through and through. And if you got his heart, then you got his blood." He grinned at me, two fangs poking over his bottom lip. "Lucky blood."

Granddad lifted his left arm and more spiders poured out, dozens of them, clattering down his fingers and onto me, spinning their webs around me, cocooning me to the chair. Granddad leaned in close and I could see his fangs grow longer, his eyes separate into sixes, his body lengthen and expand. He clacked his teeth together and lowered his head to my wrist and took it in his hands and bit—just the tiniest little nip, but it hurt.

And he drank my blood. I could feel him slurp it right out of my arm.

I felt it leaving me, power or light or life, something important that ran through my heart and veins all day. I wondered if this was it, if this would be the end of me, if Pop would rot off in jail or wherever Boss Authority had him, if there was no hope for us left.

But then Granddad clacked his fangs together twice and spat. My blood smudged the dust on the ground.

"It's tainted," he said. "This boy's been hexed."

"Hexed?" I said.

Granddad whirled around and faced down Tally, who was cowering in her chair. "Cursed! Spoilt!" he screeched, waving his hairy arms around. "You brought me a boy with hexed blood!"

"I didn't know, Granddad," she said. "He said he was Davey Boy's son. He didn't say nothing about being hexed."

Granddad coughed and spat again onto the floor. "Hexed blood, in my kitchen! Useless girl!"

He leered over her, eyes upon eyes, his fangs brushing her face. Spiders swarmed off me and scuttled over to Tally, climbing up her legs where she sat, transfixed in that chair like she was terrified for her life.

"This is the last time I let you fail me," said Granddad. "I give you one task, bring me something I can use. Something valuable. Something I can sell. And all I get are a few coins nicked from a fisherman and some brat with spoiled blood. Hexed blood is poison, don't you know that? You could have killed me! I could be a heap writhing on the floor right now, no thanks to you. I ought to give you exactly what you deserve."

"No, Granddad," said Tally, big tears running down her cheeks. "Please don't."

He lurched forward and sank his fangs into her neck. Tally screamed.

I found I could move. It must have been those spider eyes, that gaze that held me to my chair. I gathered up Pop's cards quick as I could, stuffed them in the knapsack. Tally kicked and punched at her granddad while he gouged at her with his fangs. I could have left right then. I could have sprinted out of that spider's lair and never looked back.

Maybe Tally deserved it, whatever was going to happen to her, for tricking me, for bringing me up here to have my blood sucked. But I saw how scared she looked, how terrified she was, and I started to imagine her life, right then and there. I wondered where her mom and pop were, what happened to them, how she got mixed up with this big magic spider fella. Maybe Tally's life had been one long starving struggle, an awful spider-person knocking her around all day. Maybe my life was cake compared to poor Tally's, even if she did just try to have me killed.

I don't know. It broke my heart.

I grabbed the lantern off the table and flung it right at old Granddad. It burst onto his back and his shirt exploded in flames. He shrieked this horrible bug yowl and scuttled up the wall, flaming, through a hole in the ceiling.

"Granddad!" screamed Tally. She turned to me. "What did you do to him?"

I started to reply, but then I couldn't. See, Tally's face had changed. Her eyes grew black and separated, and now there were six of them. Her arms seemed skinny and shaggy with hair, and two little fangs jutted out from her lip. She was a spider-folk, just like her granddad.

I bolted down the stairs and out into the street.

I ducked past people hawking hot foods and cheap wares, I dodged women and men street dancing while a boy scraped out a rhythm on a washboard, I tripped over a tuba player, I hopped over a foot-long rat with black bright eyes. My arm was throbbing something awful, two deep puncture holes where Tally's granddad took a nibble at me. I splashed through puddles and sprinted past old men tossing dice in an alley. I had to get back to that old lady's shack, to that pier. I'd seen some old half-rotten boats lying around, dismal and forgotten. Maybe I could borrow me a nice one, Lord willing, and I'd be able to find my own way out of Gentlesburg.

I was scared those spider-folk were after me, I was afraid they'd spin a web around me and finish the job, slurp out my blood till I was withered as jerky, all drained out and empty. I ran harder.

I started feeling woozy, the world going bright and strange. Faces changed, twisting, everyone grinning at me with big cheeks and dark scowling brows, like they were a bunch of clowns, like the town was full of circus folk and scarecrows with knives for fingers, like every person had horned ears and a lizard's tail, like their tongues were flicking in and out of their mouths like baby snakes. A man reared back and howled at the moon like he was a wolf, and a woman smiled at me with a mouth that was all teeth same as a skeleton would, like she was nothing but bones. I was running so fast I stepped on a cat's tail and tripped, nearly tumbled down, and the cat looked up at me and began to cry, big fat wet human tears, and my arm was throbbing, my arm hurt so badly.

I flopped over against a boarded-up doorway and took a deep breath, and then another, and then another. I saw the stars shining little blue eyes in the street puddles, a few feral dogs licking at the water, and I liked that, I hoped those little puppies lapped up whole galaxies while they were at it. One of the strays came up and licked my hands, and it felt crazy, like little ants crawling on my skin. A red line was streaking from my bite marks up my arm, and I wondered if now my hexed blood was poisoned with spider venom, if it would just swoll up all nasty and huge and explode on me, if I wasn't a goner already.

The stray looked up at me and panted.

"Hey pup dog," I said. "I think you might be my only friend."

He yipped happily, his eyes bright and black and knowing, the way a good dog's eyes are. I realized he was hungry then, that he was asking me for food.

"I'm sorry, pup dog," I said. "I ain't got any food for you. I ain't got hardly a scrap."

The dog yipped again, like, *That's okay, I still like you, I didn't figure you had anything anyway.* Dogs are good like that, I wager. Dogs don't know how not to love you.

I sat there sweating, my stomach starting to tighten and churn, feeling sick and fevery, like I got the flu but ten times worse. I was spider bit and ill for sure, and if these were my last stars and my last moon, I was happy they were so bright and lovely, that the moon glowed down on me with my mom's face, that the stars were a map of all the places my soul would go when it up and left my body. That was a good thought. The journey never does quite end, does it?

The dog yapped again and it was like it was saying, *Get up, Buddy. You ain't got time to die yet.*

"Okay, pup dog," I said. "If you insist."

I straggled myself to my feet and headed off toward that old lady's house, hoping something else good would work out for me. It took me a minute but I found her shack. The whole place was dark and empty, just a rotting nothing on a busted pier right on the edge of the water. It looked like the old lady had cleared out, it looked like she'd never been there at all. A dozen feral cats loped around in the darkness, their tails swishing little question marks in the air.

And then I saw it, among the heaps of old rotten wood half-sunk in the pier—an honest-to-God skiff, perfect for wallowing through swamp water. I could have shouted for joy, I would have done a dance right then and there if I hadn't been all sick from my spider-folk bite. I looked up to Heaven and I said some thank-yous, don't you doubt for one second. Somebody was looking out for me, that's for sure. Maybe that would overcome the hex on my blood and get me out of Gentlesburg in one piece. Regardless, this skiff right here was the first bit of genuine good luck I'd had in ages.

I was probably gonna have to repent a thousand times for borrowing it, but at least I wasn't stealing it. After all, I did have the intent to return the skiff, somehow, someday, right back here where I found it. Surely, that belief was somewhere in my heart.

I hunched down to loosen the knot that tied it to the dock and felt something cold slide up against my throat.

"Stay right where you are, partner," said a high ragged whisper of a voice. "Don't do nothing that would make me have to transform you into a corpse."

I felt the pointy end of another knife sticking into my back.

Well, that was the end of my good-luck streak. I figured it was the shortest durn good-luck streak in the all-time history of luck.

"Don't you move now," the voice said. I could feel the knives slide off my throat and away from my back. "Don't you even think about running. Just hold your hands behind you and I'll tie 'em up real quick-like. But if you try and run, you're a goner."

I reached my arms behind my back, just like the man said

to. I felt cold ropes wrap around my wrists too tight, the brittle cut of them on my skin. Yep, my good-luck streak had ended, so far as I was concerned.

"Now stand up and face me, little blood," said the man. "Let me look you in the eyes."

I did as I was told. It was the boy from the Skinny Yellow Dog, the magician kid with the top hat. Except that under the muddy moon and stars I could see his face was covered in white makeup, like he was some kind of actor, and underneath was all wrinkles and leathery skin. His teeth clacked in his mouth and I realized he had dentures in. His eyes were bloodshot. The suit looked ragged and old, like he'd worn it for twenty years straight. That yellow tuft of hair hung crooked under his hat. It was a wig, I realized.

This kid wasn't a kid at all. He was just an old man pretending, a short stooped old faker magician with two knives drawn and pointed at me.

"Anybody chasing after Boss Authority's got to be worth some money to him, I suppose," said the magician. "You got to be worth at least a pouch of gold, or a stake at the table."

"I don't see that I'm worth squat to him," I said, "seeing as how he don't even know that I exist. I couldn't care less about Boss Authority. I just want my daddy back."

The magician chuckled to himself, dentures going *clackety clack clack*. "If your daddy's who you said he is, then sure enough Boss Authority will want you. He'll take a special interest in you, that I guarantee."

"What's that supposed to mean?" I said.

"How much do you actually know about your daddy? Do you have any idea what kind of trouble he's in?"

I didn't say a word, because I'll be honest, I didn't have a clue. I didn't know why Boss Authority was after Pop. I didn't know a durn thing at all. I felt all dizzy and nearly puked right then on the magician's shoes.

"But I been hexed," I said. "And spider-folk bit too."

"Likely enough that is," said the magician. "That ain't any of my problem. Now hop in that skiff and let's set off now. No good keeping Boss Authority waiting, and we got us one long journey to go."

He poked at me with both of those knives, and seeing as how I didn't have much choice in the matter, I did as he said. The skiff was sturdy and good and what's more, it was new, you could tell. This was a good skiff, laid out like a birthday present for me, even though it wasn't my birthday. It was a heck of a lot better than anything my mom had given me, Lord bless her, much less Pop. And now I had to go and get kidnapped with it.

"This is my lucky day," the magician said. He whistled. "You know what I'm gonna get with all that money Boss Authority's gonna give me?"

"What's that?" I said.

My head swirling and loopy, I wanted to know. I wanted

to know what was worth turning me over to the fiercest man in the Swamplands.

"A dirigible."

"A dirigible?"

"Yes sirree," he said. "A bona fide hot-air balloon. I want to sail over all y'all's heads. I want to be flying over everybody's heads and look down over them like they're nothing, every person who ever picked on me no bigger than an ant. I been broke all my life. Short too. I want to fly. I want to be higher than the birds."

"I can kind of understand that," I said. "I've wanted to ride in a dirigible my whole life, and that's a fact."

"Oh I'll give you a ride then!" he said, all excited. "I mean, if Boss Authority doesn't"—and he drew his finger across his neck like a knife.

"Gee," I said. "Thanks. You know, if my daddy was here, rest assured he would whoop the ever-living fire out of you right now."

"That may well be," said the magician. "But the fact of the matter remains, your daddy ain't here. And I am. So what's that say about your daddy?"

I looked up at the magician, hating his guts, while he made ready to hop off the pier and onto the skiff. About midstep he stopped, his foot dangling off into the night air. His left hand was suddenly empty, that knife long gone from it. Another hand held it now, tight against his throat. He flailed with the right-hand knife and I saw the one against his throat pull tighter and a tiny trickle of blood run down onto his collar, staining his suit.

A girl's voice sounded from behind the magician.

"Drop it," she said. "Though it would be my pleasure to spill you wide open all over this pier and leave you for gator bait."

It was Tally. She'd snuck up on him and pickpocketed that knife straight out of the magician's fingers.

He dropped the other knife. It went plop in the water.

"Now spit out them false teeth of yours," she said.

He did. Tally kicked them off the pier.

"Take off your hat," she said. "I don't want to be surprised by nothing hiding underneath that."

He did. Two birds flew out from under it.

"That's a pretty good trick," said Tally. "Too bad ain't anybody ever going to see you do it again. Not in this town anyhow. You got that?"

"Durn spider-folk, you are," he said, his gums smacking. "I heard about you."

"Then you heard about my granddad, ain't you?"

The magician nodded, his eyes gone wide as a frog's.

"Skedaddle," she said. "And I'm keeping this knife to remember you by."

The magician scuttled off, his shoes pounding the pier boards before he turned a corner and was gone. Tally stood there, half spider, her six eyes staring down at me.

"You gonna let me cut them ropes off you or what?" she said.

I turned and she sliced me free.

"Thanks," I said. "Did I kill your granddad?"

"Nope," she said. "He didn't hardly catch fire. Though that don't make him any less furious at you. Or at me."

"It ain't your fault," I said. "I'm the one who chucked a lantern at him."

"And I'm the one who brought him hexed blood," she said. "That makes us about even in terms of guilt. At least in Granddad's eyes."

I lay there in the skiff, feeling about as sick as I ever could. Tally held the magician's knife in her furry hands. She climbed into the boat, hardly rocking it at all. Ol' Tally was a real pro at boats, I decided.

"You come to finish the job?" I said, my voice gone whispery and harsh from the sickness. "Get back on his good side that way?"

"Don't think there's much to finish," she said. "Granddad's venom is about the most powerful there is. 'Course, he wouldn't have spit it into you if he hadn't been so surprised by the hex in your blood. Granddad doesn't usually poison folks whose blood he draws."

"Guess I'm just that unlucky, huh?"

"I wouldn't say that." Tally spit into her palms and rubbed

them together until they formed some kind of paste, white and sticky, like a spider's web.

"Nice thing about being what I am," she said, "is that I don't just poison folks, you know? I got the cure in me too."

She rubbed the paste on my arm, right over the bite marks. It stung a bit, and I hollered out.

"Shhh, now," she said. "I know you're tougher than that."

"Trying to be."

"Trying is good enough."

Tally massaged my arm, blowing soft on it. She bent over it and I got nervous again, like she was going to bite me same as her granddad did. I tried to yank my arm back, to swat her away. Heck, I was so sick I probably moaned a little too.

"Hush already," she said. "If I wanted you dead I would have just let that magician do the job. Trust me now."

She spat into my wound and rubbed it in some more. It hurt, a whole lot, it stung and burned and was some kind of awful agony. But then the pain began to cool, to soothe, like cold water on a sunburn.

"See?" she said. "You're already feeling better."

Tally pulled a canteen of water from around her neck and offered me some. It tasted good, better than I ever thought water could taste. My head didn't hurt so bad, and I felt like some of my wits were coming back. I wasn't gonna die after all, and I was awful glad of it.

I peered at Tally closer now, her fangs, her furry arms. Nope, down deep, she was still the same Tally I first met. The same hustler, the same genius pickpocket, a low-down kid like me. What I'm trying to say is that I still liked her, despite everything. But I didn't quite trust her, and nobody can blame me for that.

"Why are you helping me?" I said.

"Because I can't stay here in Gentlesburg," she said. "Not anymore. Not with Granddad like he is. He's gotten worse, see? He used to just lock me in the wardrobe when I messed up, or maybe throw a plate at me. He never bit me with his fangs before." For a second I thought she was going to cry, if spider-folk *can* cry. But then she shook it off. "Time to hit the river."

"So you're gonna come help me find my daddy?" I said.

"Nope," she said. "But I am gonna hitch a ride into the swamp, see if I can't find me a cure."

"A cure?" I said. "Can you cure the spider out of you?"

"To be honest, I don't got a clue," she said. "But I've heard tell of mighty witches who can hex folks into dogs, or who can turn people into part fishes, with gills and everything, so they can swim underwater. Any witch strong enough to do that can surely find a fix for what's wrong with me."

I wanted to say something nice to Tally right about then, something comforting, but I was scared if I opened my mouth I was gonna puke right there in this boat.

Tally sighed.

"I'm sick of picking pockets, Buddy. I'm sick of my grand-dad, and I'm sick of this dingy spider-life in wretched old Gentlesburg. I want to be cured, Buddy. I don't want to be hexed anymore."

That I could understand perfectly, yes sir. I'd realized I must've been hexed my whole life and I hadn't hardly known it. That's why nothing had ever gone right with me. That's why I was friendless and alone, that's why Mom's bakery had burned itself down. Still, that didn't mean I needed a companion for this trip. I was hunting Pop, I was, and it was dangerous business.

"What if I say you can't come?" I croaked.

"I say you're not well enough to tell me one thing or the other," she said.

The girl had a point.

"But I thought you said you cured me."

"You ain't cured yet. I got to give you the remedy at least two more times, and that's a fact. Unless you want your arm swelling up like a bullfrog."

My stomach did a backflip and for one second my whole vision went black.

"Fine," I said. "Let's just get the heck out of Gentlesburg."

"I'll give an amen to that," said Tally. She finished untying the skiff, and we floated off, Tally rowing until the current could grab us and drag us onward. A river of clouds crossed the sky, heat lightning flickering far off. The moon was nothing but a ghost in the clouds above me, the stars lonesome notes from an old forgotten song.

It was like I could hear them sing, those stars. It was like the moon was the conductor and the rivers and waters and oceans of the world were all hollering out, the trees too, singing every far-off note the stars wrote in the sky.

"That's just the venom working itself out your system," said Tally.

Well that was something, wasn't it? I hadn't even known I was speaking out loud.

9

WE FLOATED DOWN THE RIVER, following that
slow and steady tug swampward. Tally kept the skiff straight,
rowing when we needed, but mostly the river did the work.
It struck me then that water is the most powerful thing, just
like Pop said, water running like blood to the heart of the
earth. But what about love then? Mom believed love was
more powerful, didn't she? Who would win in a contest,
water or love, that's what I wanted to know.

Tally dipped her hand into the river and then laid it on
my forehead. It felt cool in the night air, it felt like healing.
"You just rest up now. We'll be in the swamp in no time."

I slept then, I think. Or maybe I just dreamed. Fever
will do that to you, make you dream with your eyes open,
cast your thoughts big and loud up in the sky above. I saw

monkeys dangling in the trees, their eyes red as fire, speaking in tongues like at a tent revival. I saw clouds like warships, big sixteen-sailed battle boats armed with cannons and blood-starved pirates ready to burn and plunder. I saw the ghosts of old women wash their dark hair in the river. They had no eyes, just empty black sockets, and they smiled at me like sad friends at a funeral. The trees began to lean in closer, to dangle their gray scraggly beards like old wizards peering down at us. Snakes slithered across the water like miracles, and there were all manner of bugs—biting sucking buzzing bugs, bugs everywhere. The swamp was alive tonight, don't you doubt that. The swamp was so full of life I couldn't see how there was any room for us, for me and my new pal Tally to fit.

"Hush up now," she said, "just rest."

And I did, I fell right to sleep.

I woke up here and there, in fits and starts. Once when the moon was high I woke and nearly yelped out. Tally was in her full spider face, hunching up in the boat, all six eyes awake and watching. Around us flashed gold and silver lights that would blink and vanish, as if beckoning us to follow.

"What are those?"

"Fairy lights," she said. "You follow them off into the marsh and you'll never come back."

Her voice shook, like she was scared, like this fierce half

spider with her fangs was trembling in our little boat. What could scare someone like Tally?

"Quiet," she said. "They're listening."

"Who's listening?"

But Tally wouldn't say a word.

I imagined all that could live in this swamp, ghost hermits and old dead monks ringing their bells, their cathedrals all long sunk into the muck. Kids who wandered in this swamp and got lost, turned around, folks who never made their way out, who wander still, though they'd long left their bodies behind. Not to mention all the scaly hidden creatures with bright blinking eyes hid deep in the dark and wild and muck.

"Be quiet already," whispered Tally. "Lest you want to call them right to us. Lest you never want to leave the Swamplands alive."

I guessed I was talking out loud again. I guessed I couldn't tell a difference between my brain and mouth right about then. Something hollered in the woods, a high mournful yip like an old sad song, an echo of a song sung a thousand years ago that's just been lingering around, singing to itself. Tally bristled, and every brown spider hair on her body bristled.

"You see that?" said Tally. She pointed up to a tree limb above us. A daisy chain of fingerbones dangled down, hung on it like a garland. There were skulls fit into the notches of a cypress tree.

"The Creepy," she said.

"There ain't such thing as the Creepy," I said. "My daddy told me."

Tally looked down at me, all six of her eyes wild and black and reflecting moonlight.

"If I were you," she said, "I'd start wondering about what my daddy said that was true and what he said that wasn't."

10

I WOKE UP AND IT was bright noon. Tally looked just
like a normal girl right then—only two eyes, not a fang in
sight—slumped over and snoozing in the front of the skiff.
The day was hot and the swamp water glistened gold with
sunlight. Damselflies touched water and danced away, and
big fat lily pads floated on by. I saw a log sticking out of the
water with a pile of turtles on it, one on top of the other, like
a circus trick. One of them opened his mouth and gawked at
me. It was a papa turtle I was pretty sure.

"Howdy, papa turtle," I said out loud.

Tally jerked awake and snatched up an oar like she was
about to smack me with it.

"Good lord, Buddy," she said, "you scared the dickens out
of me."

The sunlight glistened off the dew-wet leaves above us and it was like a spill of gold coins jangled in the breeze.

"It's funny," I said. "I never thought about the swamp being pretty. Guess I was too young to think stuff like that last time I was here. But it is, you know? It's so calm and quiet, at least in the daytime. Peaceful even."

"That's because you don't see what's happening underneath," she said. "There's a whole world of critters eating other critters just below us, not making hardly a ripple. You call that beautiful?"

"Yeah," I said. "I think I do."

"Suit yourself," Tally said.

My stomach growled something awful. I realized I hadn't eaten since Granddad's stew.

"Think we can stop and find some food?" I said.

"Not on your life."

"Why not?"

"Lest you forget, we're on the run."

That made me pretty glum, if you want to know the truth about it. I didn't want Tally to know that, so I tried to be brave about it.

"Naw, you're right," I said. "We got to keep going if we're gonna find Pop in time. The sooner we find Pop the sooner we can get back to our house on the river and everything will be fine and good again. Once I tell him I been hexed, he'll go straightaway and fix that. And I'm sure he'll know how to find a cure for you no problem. You're gonna love Pop. Everybody does."

"I'm sure I will," she said. Tally spat into the water. "I'm sure I'll be durn glad to meet him."

"What are you so sore about?" I said.

"Well, if you want me to be honest," she said.

"Oh, I do."

"A'ight then, I'll tell you. One, I'm hungry and we're floating down the durn swamp through goblin territory and I don't know what else, all to try and find your daddy who's probably locked up in Boss Authority's jail by now. Two, you burned the hair off Granddad's back and he's mad enough to kill you and me both about it. Third, you're so excited to see your pop, but guess what? I don't even know my daddy. Not my mom either. They ditched me when I was a kid, on account of how I got the spider-blood in me, same as my granddad. My mom didn't inherit it, because she's beautiful and lucky and all them other things. But me? I got stuck with it. And they sent me to live with ornery old Granddad and I been robbing and stealing for him ever since. All because of this stupid spider-blood. It ain't even my fault."

"Can I be honest with you real quick?" I said. "I think you being spider-folk is amazing."

"Amazing how?"

"I mean, you healed me didn't you? And the way you looked last night? All battle ready and tough? My lord, who would ever want to mess with me when I got you around. And you're the best pickpocket I ever seen, no question about that. You're the fastest, smartest kid I ever met in my life." I was scared to say the next part, but I figured I would go ahead and try it anyway. "And you're my friend, ain't you?"

Tally nodded.

"I never really had one of those before. My bad-luck blood always made me ruin it somehow. Like this one kid, Freddie George Persons, who lived down the street from me? He was outside bopping a sheep's bladder around pretty good. I never much cared for sheep's bladders, but he was having fun, and I wasn't more than seven years old. So I figure maybe I can run out and play with him too.

"So I ask him, 'Freddie George, can I bounce that sheep's bladder?' 'Okay,' he says, and bops it over to me. I promise you right now, I didn't so much as lay a finger on it before that bladder up and shriveled. I mean deflated flat. Freddie George never talked to me again. That's how it goes with everybody. That's what happens every time I try and do anything. I mean heck, I was only with Pop for one night and he got kidnapped. Nothing to blame for that but myself and my durn hexed blood."

"Well here's to finding a cure for the both of us," said Tally.

"I'm all in on that," I said. "Just hope we can find some lunch on the way too."

Some big old seabirds flew over our heads, squawking up a storm. Somewhere a frog leapt out and belly flopped in the water. All of nature was out and having a durn good time. At least a much better time than I was. Probably eating too, frogs eating up flies, mosquitoes sucking up blood, gators chomping on fish heads. Every last critter with a bellyful, except me. I was hungry and thirsty and I didn't dare drink any swamp water. I heard all kinds of stories about what would happen if you did that. Lily pads would sprout in your stomach. You'd open your mouth and a swarm of mosquitoes would come buzzing out. Worst of all, you might swallow frog eggs and be burping up toads the rest of your life.

Also I found a tick big as a blueberry on my noggin. Must have been there for days but I was too preoccupied to notice. Tally plucked it off for me with her fingernails. She's a pro, even got the head out, no problem, so the wound wouldn't get infected. I figured she'd be sympathetic toward ticks, her being part spider and all, but when I mentioned it she stuck her tongue out at me.

"I'm just gonna go ahead and pretend you didn't say that to me."

"What?" I said. "What did I do?"

If there's one thing I've learned in this life it's that I'm aces at saying the exact durn wrong thing all the time.

Tally didn't hardly talk to me for a whole hour after that. Sitting in a boat with someone all day, trading off rowing until your hands get blistery when you're hungry and they won't even talk to you is pretty tough. You just don't know what to do with yourself. I couldn't figure out what in the heck this Boss Authority had to do with Pop. I figured maybe it was something about a Parsnit game gone wrong, knowing Pop. I bet Pop whooped him so bad Boss Authority sent spies after him, trying to make Pop pay for embarrassing him. But why did Pop know the two guys that came after him? It was too much for me to figure out right now. So I pulled out Pop's Parsnit deck and laid out each card one at a time, peering close at each one, trying to will myself into them, like a real Parsnit player does. I started learning Parsnit. I mean really learning it, studying the cards, listening for their stories. Like how the Sleepy Town's got a chimney just like Mom's house, or how the Bramble has the feel of the woods not a mile from Collardsville.

"You got a card missing," said Tally.

"What?" I said. "No I don't."

"Do too," said Tally. "I've watched you flip through that deck about a dozen times, and I tell you there's one card missing."

Then I knew it. I hadn't seen the Red Bride anywhere. She was the most powerful card in the whole game. She could evoke Oration so mighty whole duels turned whenever she popped up. But the Red Bride was being shy right now. I shuffled through the deck twice. No matter how many times I flipped the cards, she just wasn't there.

"Hold up a minute," said Tally. She wiggled her fingers over the cards and then went stiff with them, like each one was a separate magic wand. Then she snatched a card from the middle of the deck.

"Gotcha!" she said. "Now hold still, ain't any use in getting away now."

The Red Bride was there all right, her gown gone a dark blood crimson, might and power in her eyes, like she didn't need nobody else, like she could maybe marry lightning or maybe a house on fire, but anything else would be too weak, too tame for her. I'd always been a bit in awe of the Red Bride myself.

But something seemed a little off about her now. Her gown hung limp and the spark was out of her eyes, her shoulders sagged. Worst of all, there was a long black scar over the card, as if someone had lit it on fire. I ran my hand over it, but it was smooth. The scar was something deep in the magic of the card.

Tally whistled.

"I'm sorry," I said, "I don't understand. What does that

mean? Why's the card all messed up?"

"It means your daddy played a Parsnit duel," said Tally, "a long fearsome terrible one." She looked up at me, eyes dark and black and blinking. "And he lost."

"He lost?"

I couldn't hardly believe it. My daddy losing at Parsnit? It just didn't happen.

"Yep."

The Red Bride seemed about to burst into tears so I slid her back in the deck, so she could be alone again.

"Could that be the source of my hex? All my problems?" I said.

"It's possible," said Tally. "I'm no witch, but I've known a fair share of them. From what I gather, magic ain't an exact science. It's approximate at best. You send your dust out in the world, say a spell or two, and watch the threads of fate tangle. Sometimes they tangle in your favor. Who can say how magic works, or how it doesn't?"

"Lot of help that does me," I said.

"Since you're all healed up," she said, "how about you take a turn rowing."

"Fine, fine," I said. "But it'd be a heck of a lot easier if I wasn't so durn hungry."

Tally grinned at me then, a little spider-fanged smile. She let her spit dangle down and twirled it with her fingers, same as she did when she gave me the remedy. Except it was spooling differently this time, becoming a slender, taut thread between her fingers, almost translucent. I could only see it when the sun hit it just right.

"Whatcha making?" I said.

"Fishing line," she said. "Think you can find me a hook?"

We were moving so slow in that mucky green swamp water that it was no problem for me to reach out and catch hold of a twiny catbrier vine and cut an extra-mean-looking thorn off it. While I whittled that thorn sharp, Tally snatched a handful of crickets out of a passing spiderweb stretched between two low-hanging cypress limbs. I thought about making some dumb joke about her stealing from her own people but I was afraid she would take offense. The way she smirked to herself, though, I figured she was thinking the same thing. We hooked a cricket right through the thorn and dropped it in the water.

It took a while, hours even, but eventually Tally caught us a catfish, a long-whiskered wriggling sucker that Tally yanked into the boat and I bashed in the head with an oar. After that, Tally tried to get me to fish, but I wouldn't dare.

"Why?" she said. "Is it because my webbing spooks you?"

"Naw," I said. "It's my bad luck. Last time I went fishing the only thing I hooked was a snapping turtle the size of a bear. It like to took my hand off." I sighed. "Fish always get away from me, right when I pull them out of the water. Yes ma'am, letting me fish with your line is a bona fide waste of time."

What I did do was stretch out on that skiff and take a good gander at my surroundings. I hadn't been home to the swamp in ages, and oh my was it ever good to be back. I watched an egret swoop into the water and come up with a beak full of fish. I watched a woodpecker hammer away at a maplewood tree. I saw a meadow of yellowtops growing right up out of the water. I saw water bugs float themselves like pirate ships across the belly of the murk. I saw blackjack vines wriggle same as if they were snakes, you couldn't half tell them apart. I saw swamp lilies so beautiful I wanted to yank them up and make a bouquet out of them.

"Now we got to stop," said Tally, "so we can cook and clean this sucker."

I nodded.

"But let's be quick about it," she said. "We're after your daddy, ain't we? Can't let him get too far ahead of us."

We pulled over on a sandbar, a small island rising out of the muck. It took a while but I gathered a few limbs from a dead, lightning-struck tree and built a fire, while Tally cleaned the fish. It wasn't much divided between us, but at least it was a mouthful or two. I guessed that was better than nothing.

* * *

We drifted on and on, sometimes Tally rowing and sometimes me, not seeing a single durn sight of Pop. We passed
some stilt houses here and there, windows shut tight, doors
barred, little eyes peeping from behind the curtains. Folks
were watching, and that was a fact. Wary is what they were.
One old man stayed seated on his front porch with a rifle
trained on us.

"Howdy," I said.

He grunted at me and spat in the swamp water.

We kept on our way.

"Folks sure aren't too friendly out here," I said.

"Looks to me like they're scared," said Tally.

"Of what?" I said. I tried to laugh a little. "The Creepy?"

Tally didn't say a word.

By midafternoon, we still hadn't seen hide nor hair of
Pop. I was getting worried. We passed another one of those
bone garlands dangling from way up high in an oak tree. I
still didn't believe in the Creepy, but whatever made those
things sure wasn't up to any good. It was bad enough to be
worried about my pop without having to worry about myself
and Tally in the meanwhile.

What was undeniable was the sunset, how it was able to
change the swamp, to turn it all honey colored and lit alive.
That was some magic we could all agree on. Pinks and golds,

like a painter's bucket upturned and spilled itself all over the waters. We could have been in a king's tomb of gold, a forest of jewels, of glowing swamp cat's eyes and the scaly glimmer of a snake slithering across the water.

Tally sat upright.

"Do you feel that?" she said.

The water exploded with fish then, the silver-bright flicker of fish scales as they flung themselves out of the murk and over our skiff, flying they were, popping out of the water like corn kernels on a kettle, bands of jewelry sailing wild over our heads and vanishing with a splash back to where they came from. It was like they were playing, these flying fish were, like it was the greatest joy in the whole world to be a fish and spend all day trying to be a bird. The way the sunset caught them midair and turned them to gold.

It was the most beautiful thing I'd ever seen in my whole life.

It's strange, I guess, to feel as happy as I was feeling right then, even though I'd left my mom at home and my daddy was off kidnapped by lowlifes. But it was true. I *did* feel happy, I felt joyful and wild and free, and worried and fearful too, scared we were too late to help Pop, scared that we'd never make it out of the Swamplands alive.

I can't say it makes much sense, to feel two completely different feelings at once. But life doesn't make much sense either, does it? Not in my experience. You can save all the making sense for stories, for tales spun from Parsnit cards and wild yarns whispered around campfires.

Real life is too big and weird and confusing for something so simple as making sense.

II

NIGHT CAME ON FAST. ME and Tally slept in shifts, which meant neither of us hardly caught a wink. Way past midnight and creeping up on morning time I was finally drifting off into some weird dream about Mom making a pie out of a one-eyed pigeon when Tally shook me awake.

"Look," she whispered.

Ahead of us glimmered a small fire burning on a patch of dry land that rose like a giant elbow from the water. Two figures were gathered around the fire, cooking something, I could smell it. It smelled awful. Tally and I ducked low in the boat, hoping we would drift past in the fog and the darkness and no one would notice, they wouldn't see a thing of us.

It worked. We passed them by no problem, we drifted until they were far out of earshot. Tally slumped over, all relaxed and pleased with herself.

That was a close one.

But I didn't feel that way, not one bit. It was a missed opportunity is what I was thinking.

"I got to find out who they are," I said. "They might know something about my pop."

I didn't know why, but I had a feeling about those two. It was something bothering me deep in my guts.

"Buddy, that is about the dumbest idea I've ever heard in my whole durn life."

"Probably is," I said. "But I'm feeling better now, half-healed-up thanks to you, and Pop's life is at stake. I'd do anything to save my daddy, and you know it. So what I got to do is this."

I untied my boots then and slung them around my neck. Last thing you want to do is hop into water with your boots still on. That's how folks drown, or best case that's how folks lose their boots and have to wander around barefoot the whole rest of the journey. Tally rowed us over to a big cypress tree and half docked us there, tying a rope around a knotty root sticking up in the water. We were lucky we didn't get stuck right there, we were, seeing as how shallow the swamp could get. Maybe what I was doing was brick dumb, or maybe I'd find some folks that could help me. Who knew? But it was Pop we were talking about, and Pop was worth the risk. So I took a deep breath and then

I hopped. I held myself close and tried to splash as little as possible, and when I went under, it was so deep my feet couldn't touch, and my head popped up into the air and I was treading water.

I swam my way toward the two men, paddling quiet as I could. My feet could touch bottom now, the marshy, soggy earth. They sank deep but I could walk, and boy did it feel good to touch ground again. I was waist-deep in the water when my knee kicked a log real hard and I tried to step over it but the log rose in the water, it broke the surface with its green armored scales tough as tree bark and eight foot long.

It wasn't any log. It was a gator.

The gator opened its jaws and it was like the mouth of the river opened up, it was like a sinkhole widened to swallow me whole.

I clapped my hands over my mouth and stood dead still as I possibly could while that gator circled me. I could feel its rough gator skin slide across my back, feel its tail whip my knees, until it circled me whole and faced me, eye to eye, its snout not one inch from my nose.

That's when I realized it wasn't any normal gator. No sir. This gator had one yellow eye right in the center of its forehead. I stared at it long and slow, and it stared right back at me with that forehead eye, like it was reading my mind, like it was telling me some deep dark truth I needed to know for the whole rest of my life. I started to say my prayers right then, oh boy did I, waiting for it to chomp me to bits.

But the gator lowered into the water until its eye vanished and its back vanished and then it was invisible, hidden deep in the muck. I felt a whoosh of water and then it was gone, disappeared into the swamp. I realized the water could be full of one-eyed gators. The swamp water could be full of anything and I wouldn't hardly know it. It was one big murky mystery, the swamp was, and it always would be forever.

I paddled closer, not ten feet from the men now, the fog like swamp's breath, me nestled deep in it. The moon broke through the clouds and cast a glow down on the men's faces and I yelped I was so excited.

It was Cecily Bob and Mr. Hugo crouched there by the fire. It looked like they were cooking a rat. They were looking my way.

"You hear something, Mr. Hugo?"

"Aye, sir, I heard something, I did."

"One of them big-tusked pigs you think?"

"Sounded more like a human to me, it did."

"A human you say? Could it be the man himself?"

"If only we were so lucky, Cecily Bob. But something tells me we are not."

"Aye," said Cecily Bob. They peered out into the gloom. "I don't see nothing. Perhaps it's passed on."

"That would be my wager."

"Aye. Our poor luck continues."

"Does it ever, Cecily Bob."

They looked sad, hunched over like too big gangly vultures around that fire. But if they were there, where was Pop? What happened to him?

"Do we suppose he drowned then?" said Cecily Bob.

"That would be my supposition," said Mr. Hugo.

Drowned? My daddy drowned? How?

"I say we tell the truth. That I was rowing and you was sleeping and he was all tied up and he rolled himself right out the boat, that's what we tell them. He rolled himself right out and splashed into the water."

"And what say ye when Boss Authority asks for a body?"

"We say the swamp swallowed him whole, that's what we say."

It couldn't be true. Pop couldn't have died. Not like this. He wouldn't have drowned, there's no way. Big tears were rolling hot down my face and I kept both hands over my mouth to keep from crying, to keep from weeping all over everything. I was too late. My daddy was long dead. I was just so durn sad you could have chucked me into the water and let me drown and I wouldn't hardly have fought you at all.

"Then what say ye about these ropes we found," said Mr. Hugo, "cut clean?"

"Are they not the ropes that bound the old fellow?"

"Aye, they are."

"Then we don't say nothing."

The ropes were cut? They couldn't find the body? Then maybe Pop wasn't dead. Maybe he somehow broke free, and he was hiding somewhere in the swamp. I bet he was already making his way back upriver to check on me. I bet he was already scrambling to send word to me that he was good and alive. Or maybe he was sitting pretty somewhere, planning his revenge, plotting his payback to Mr. Hugo and Cecily Bob and even Boss Authority himself.

Pop wasn't dead, not a chance, no sirree. Pop was just getting started. I was so happy I could have danced. I could have fallen to my knees and shouted hallelujahs all day.

I had to get back to the skiff and tell Tally. I kicked soft and quiet as I could through the swamp water and muck, hoping there weren't any snakes slithering, hoping no weird fanged fishes darted underneath me, hoping I wouldn't stub my toe on a snappy turtle or kick a catfish spine by accident. I'd seen those suckers stick a man and the wound gets all swoll up and purple and you're useless for a durn week. That would be just my luck, wouldn't it? Find out Pop ain't dead and first thing I do is get skewered by a catfish.

But I made it safe and sound back to the skiff and I climbed back up in it and Tally untied the rope.

"Pop escaped!" I said.

"Shhh!" said Tally. "We're not quite far enough away yet. They'll hear you."

"Sorry," I whispered. "But Pop flew the coop! They think he drowned, but I doubt it. I bet he's somewhere out here in this swamp now, plotting his revenge. Yes sir, I bet my daddy right now is planning how to pay Boss Authority back for what he's done. I bet he's watching you and me right now, trying to figure out the best time to hop out and save us, to bring us right where he is. Yessirree, I tell you, my pop ain't worried about a thing."

"Keep it down or we won't be getting anywhere except dead," she whispered. "And I'm about durn sick of rowing. You seem healthy now, and I'm ready for a rest."

"Fine, fine," I said, and reached for the oars. But then I felt something weird under my shirt. I looked under the collar, and there they were: three thumb-sized leeches latched onto my skin, sucking my blood, hanging on for dear life.

That did it. I screamed like a baby.

I heard a holler back from Mr. Hugo and Cecily Bob's camp. My yelp had got their attention, and that's a fact. I could see skinny Cecily Bob holding a lantern high, scanning the swamp for us, Cecily Bob's and Mr. Hugo's faces turned my way. They'd seen me, there was no question about that.

I snatched the oars and started rowing.

I rowed past cypress knees poking up bald through the muck.

I rowed past tree stumps and under limbs and dodged snakes dangling like poison fruit. I bumped a dead hollow oak and a funnel of bats burst out from it, high and black and swirling like a tornado in reverse. Tally kept glancing behind us, but I didn't even need to look. I knew Mr. Hugo and Cecily Bob were gaining ground.

We came up on a tangle of trees buried deep in the fog and muck. The moss hung curtain thick down to the water.

"In there!" said Tally, and I tried to angle us through the knees and roots until we were hidden safe behind that moss curtain, in a circle of fat trees, some hollowed out and leering down over us.

We stayed dead still, Tally holding my hand, the two of us crouched and quiet in the bottom of the boat. The tree swaddled us with its moss, big limbs draped around us like a giant wretched mother's arms, bony and gaunt, bugs crawling all over them. The water was grayer and murkier here, it swirled in a baby little whirlpool that kept bumping the skiff into the trees. The trees were something else too, the bark carved on by human hands, symbols and scratch marks like how you figure a witch's spell book looks. Above us dangled bones clacking together like wind chimes, another daisy chain of digit bones, jawless skulls wedged between branches and in the knots of trees, gaping at us, all those empty eye sockets watching.

"Where are we?" I whispered, and Tally just looked at

me, eyes all big and scared.

Cecily Bob and Mr. Hugo rowed right by us, their lantern light casting us deeper into the shadow of the trees. They passed so close the moss swooshed in their wake. All the time calling, "Here, little boy! Here, little fella! We know where your daddy is, we do. Come on out!"

How do they know about me? I wondered. Was it because I came chasing after them at Pop's house? Was it because of how he yelled when they blew my boat up? Did Pop think I was dead?

They came to the circle of trees where we were hidden.

"That's the Creepy's lair it is," said Mr. Hugo. "I ain't going in there."

"If that's where the kid went," said Cecily Bob, "I reckon him a goner already."

"Aye," said Mr. Hugo. "Not much human left to the fella, is there? Come on, let's get back to hunting the father."

And they rowed themselves away.

"We did it," I whispered. "Come on, Tally, let's get out of here."

I heard a splash right next to us, on the starboard side. That's when I realized Tally wasn't holding my hand anymore.

The boat was empty except for me.

"Tally?" I whispered. Then louder, who cares if I got caught. "Tally. Tally! Where are you?"

"Shhh now, child," hissed a voice in my ears. I could smell its breath, all ripe and rotted things. "We mustn't say a word."

All those skulls staring down at me, green with grime and mold, jaws gone like they were laughing so hard they just fell off and sloshed into the water. The moon a low glow on the horizon, morning still hours off. *My luck, my luck.*

I felt a cold, wet hand grip the back of my neck and yank me, and down, down I plunged into the water as I was dragged under.

12

I CAME TO IN A dark cave with one burning torch lodged in a nook in the wall. All around me water dripped in the darkness. I couldn't see a thing, just the flickers of that one little fire. I yanked the torch from the wall and realized its handle was made of bone. I heard scuttling noises in the ground beneath me, felt my feet crunching on something. I looked down at the halo of light around my feet, and it was bones, human bones, legs and skulls and teeth and fingers. Everywhere I stepped they crunched under my feet.

"Tally?" I called into the darkness. "Tally, where are you?"

I bumped something on the ground, something soft. It groaned.

I bent down and in the torchlight saw it was Tally. She was alive, she was. I tried to drag her up to her feet.

"Come on now," I said. "We got to move."

"I wouldn't bother," rasped a voice out of the darkness. I whirled the torch around, but I couldn't see anything. The voice echoed throughout the cave, it could have been coming from anywhere. "You mustn't leave now. You can't."

"Oh yeah?" I said, trying to sound all brave. "Watch us."

"I can see you quite clearly," said the voice. I felt its breath right on my ear. "It's you who cannot see me."

I swung the torch behind me and heard a scattering of bones. Laughter bounced along the cave walls.

"Buddy?" It was Tally, she was getting up. "Where are we?"

"We're in a cave," I said. "Something's dragged us down here."

"The Creepy," she said.

"I told you already, there ain't any such thing as a Creepy," I said. "Pop said so."

I heard something scuttle at my feet. I swung the light toward the sound. A face stared back at me, no more than an inch from mine. Teeth yellow, cracked, and broken, hair scraggled down past its shoulders. In the torchlight its eyes burned black.

I screamed and dropped the torch. It glowed dimly on the cave floor. I grabbed a hand and it was warm and furry, it was Tally's, it had to be, she'd gone full spider. At least now we could fight. At least now we stood a chance.

"Spider-folk?" said the voice. "I thought they'd long died out. I thought they were just a myth."

"Think again," said Tally. "Think about how bad it'll hurt when I sink my fangs into that scrawny neck of yours."

That high wild cackling. "Oh you children are a delight. I haven't had so much fun in ages. Oh I haven't spoken with the living in so long."

I snatched the torch back up again, burning my palm a little.

"You stay back," I said. "I'm warning you. I've seen what her poison can do to a body, even a fella like you. Trust me, it ain't pretty."

"You misunderstand, child," he said. "The living have no fear of me, not at all. It's the dead I hunger for. And the dead fear no one."

He lingered just in the place where the torchlight faded, so I could see him a little. A man, or something like one, his face gray and wrinkled, his body skinny, so thin you could count his ribs, you could see every knot in his bones. His skin seemed sick, waterlogged, like if you ran your hand over his arm it would peal off in patches. He hunched down on all fours, his body shimmery and wet, dressed all in rags.

"But you're the Creepy," said Tally. "I've heard stories about you."

"If that is the name by which they call me," he said, "then I suppose the name to be true. Though I had another name once, I did. I still do, sometimes, when I'm asleep. That's when I have a name, when I'm dreaming, when best I can remember, when I can still believe it to be so."

He gestured a bone-skinny arm around the cave walls.

"This is my home, where I hide," he said. "It hurts me when folks look upon me, when their eyes fall upon me. It hurts me for them to see. And the light burns me. I come out only when I am called."

"And who calls you?" I said.

"The bodies call me," he said, his nostrils flaring. "The blood calls me. I can smell the blood, I can feel it when it touches the water, I can feel my heart beat with the dead pulse of it."

He scuttled around on all fours, some long gangly insect creature.

"I am shunned by the living, yes, I am the most lonely of all people, though the living have no fear of me. But the dead welcome me. They call themselves to me. And I minister to them."

"How can you minister to a dead body?" said Tally.

"As vultures minister to the dead, and flies and worms, as all of nature does. I clean them down to bones. I prepare them for the earth. My hands are the last to touch the body, my eyes are the last to see it. That is my blessing and my curse. No one cares about the bodies save I, and I care the most."

"The bones everywhere," I said. "The wind chimes, the skulls. Did you make all those?"

"Aye," he said. "They're mine, all of them."

"But why?" I said.

"Have you seen a burial in the swamp?" he said. "They throw the body down, and it sinks. The mud swallows it whole, that's what people think. But the bodies bubble up, they do, they float to the surface. Here and there, where no one would think to look. But I find them, I smell them, I can sense the water ripple beneath them. Can't you feel how lonesome a body is underwater? Can't you feel how forlorn its bones become? Why not make a beautiful something out of them? Why not give them a voice, make them sing like these wind chimes sing? Why not make them look on and smile, like my skulls do? They're my art, these dead bodies."

"But is it true, all the stories?" whispered Tally. "Do you . . . do you eat them?"

"The hunger calls to me," he said, "and I must obey."

"Buddy," whispered Tally. "We need to go, and now."

"No, no, children," said the Creepy. "You misunderstand. I saved you. I saved your lives." He looked dead into my eyes. "I saved you like your father was unable to save me."

My heart thudded hard and loud in my chest. Despite myself I leaned in closer to him and tried to meet his black-eyed stare.

"You knew my daddy?" I said.

"Yes, child," said the Creepy. "I knew him very, very well. Come, sit down. I have a story to tell, and it's been long since anyone but the bones have heard it."

The Creepy beckoned to us in the darkness. Boy, did I not want to follow him anywhere down this dark cave. But what else was I going to do right now? Besides, I wanted to know about my daddy. I wanted to know what Boss Authority wanted with Pop. So I took a deep brave breath and I stepped forward. The torch revealed a few seat-sized rocks amidst the bones. Tally and I sat, wary, ready to spring up and go, ready to take off running the moment things got weird. Or weirder, rather.

"Strange tidings, a tale of wickedness, it is," said the Creepy. "A tale of deceit. Your father, Buddy. Yes your father, the deceitfulest of all."

"Watch your mouth about my daddy," I said.

"Your mouth? Watch your mouth?" he said, cackling. "I would be more afraid of my mouth, and what it could do to your bones. Oh children, I would slurp the marrow from them, I would lap up every drop of your blood. It would fill me, yes it would. I would be satisfied."

"I thought you didn't eat the living?" said Tally.

"I don't, I don't," said the Creepy. "Oh but just a snap of your neck and you would be mine, and your bones would be mine. It would be so very easy."

He growled and spat again.

"But I won't do it. No I won't, I will not, I wouldn't dare. Because there is still hope, you see? There is always hope. Even for me. Even for the miserablest likes of me."

The Creepy grew quiet a moment, thoughtful, as though each word spoken caused him pain. I could tell Tally wanted to leave, but I gripped her hand tight, hoping she understood how important this was to me. Maybe the Creepy could explain to me what happened to Pop. Maybe he could even tell me why Mom had taken me and left in the first place.

"We were five, yes always there were the five of us," said the Creepy. "I was your father's friend. Sinclair, that was my name, do you remember me, child? Do you remember Sinclair in his glory?"

For the most part I couldn't recall Pop's friends from when I was a kid, since he mostly kept me separate from all his and Mom's business. But I did think I remembered a tall man, with long blond hair. A brave man, and strong, who smiled all the time, who used to toss me in the air and catch me. I was pretty sure his name had been Sinclair. There were others too—a tall witch-woman, a short man—but I remembered Sinclair the best. I remembered him laughing, I remember a great booming laugh, a laugh that made everyone else want to laugh along. But how could this shivering creature before me be the same person?

"Yes, he remembers me, the boy does. He remembers me well." And Sinclair smiled a little sadly at that.

"The five. Myself, your father, Marina—watch her, boy, should you see her, as there be no more powerful witch that walks the earth than Marina dear, not that ever I have seen—Samantha Annie, and little Bobby Felix. Samantha Annie, yes, that's your mother, child, did you know? Five we were, the best of friends, and never to be separated."

Sinclair's eyes caught a flicker of torchlight and brightened a little, and it was as if some kind of joy crept into his face right then.

"Parsnit was our game. It was the cards, the magic of the cards. It was how we made our living, running the tables from the smallest tavern all the way to Baudelaire Quatro's Place. You have heard of Mr. Quatro, have you not?"

"A little," I said. "He runs the most famous Parsnit hall in the swamp."

"Indeed, child." Sinclair's eyes grew wide and he stared me deep in my own. "Though the hall has changed significantly, as has Mr. Quatro himself. Your father would not recognize the place were he to lay eyes upon it, so much has it changed. You would be wise not to meddle with Mr. Quatro. Even Marina fears magic such as that, gruesome it is, unwholesome. As am I! Yes, as am I!"

Sinclair snatched a fresh femur bone from the cave floor and split it over his knee and began to gnaw the marrow out from the center. He spat out a chunk of gristle and spoke.

"We played the game well, and the game sustained us.

Often we weren't above hijacking a trader's longboat, or raiding some wayward boat fool enough to wind its way into our lands, all of it was ours, everything that touched the swamp waters. Those were happy times, I recall." He shuddered, the bone shard slipping from his fingers. "Famous times, yes. My days in the light, those were."

"Then how did you become, well . . . ," said Tally.

"Times changed, they always do, they always will. Time is disobedient to us, children, we are time's plaything, we are all shaped by it. Changed we are, diminished."

I heard bats flutter above us, their chirp and call. I wondered what all lived down here, in Sinclair's caves. I wondered where they all led to, all the secret tunnels and passageways, how many places in the swamp he could reach, how he could appear probably anywhere.

"But this is not my tale, no, not truly," said Sinclair. "It is Little Bobby Felix's story, and what he became. Who he became. Do you remember Bobby Felix, child? He was the weakest of us, the smallest, but he was one of ours. Our friend. And we shared all we had with him."

"He was the short fella, right?" I said. "I think I remember him."

"Yes, the boy remembers," said Sinclair. "A gentle soul, so I thought, for a time. And yet little Bobby Felix wasn't content being Bobby Felix, the weakest of us, the least mighty. He started collecting, gathering little magics. Totems, he called them, each one carrying with it some strange power. The pinky finger of a child saint, a stolen lock of hair from a Dolly Witch, the left fang of the last of the spider-folk."

Tally flinched backward and I held her hand tight.

"I thought they were all gone, spider-folk. Very valuable you are, coveted, especially by the likes of Bobby Felix. He sought such trifles out, such magical trinkets, and other things: forbidden books, the scrolls written in bark on the oldest trees in the swamp, the whispered mysteries of the bird songs, the code hidden in the lightning bugs' blink. Power was what he wanted, and power he got. He cut his own left hand off, little Bobby Felix did, and he had it dried and shrunk. He kept it in a jar, he did, and it still moved, it stayed alive, I saw it twitching on a shelf one night, saw it with my own eyes. In its place he fixed a hand of iron, of clockwork.

"I remember the night he showed his new metal fist to us first. Little Bobby Felix strode into your father's house with that hand, wicked magic it was, and ghastly. The great witch Marina fumed, she screamed and hollered and cursed him. But your mother—a mighty witch in her own right, though of a different sort than Marina—she knew, she understood. She stayed quiet, Samantha Annie, and afraid."

There was no way. My mom, a witch? Was it even possible?

"Bobby Felix began to change soon after that. He'd

disappear weeks on end, come back with some other piece of magic, some mystical tattoo snaking around his little arm. It wasn't long before Bobby Felix found himself a partner. A woman named Drusilla Fey, a dreaded witch. Pretty she was, silver-haired, could have been twenty, could have been two hundred years old, how would we know? Sneaky, duplicitous, and yet she played the lady. Proper, mincing around our Parsnit halls as if the floors would dirty her shoes. Yes, she'd play the lady prim and proper until her fingernails came out, until she wanted blood. You ever meet her, you'll understand right quick, children. Your mother, Buddy, she hated Drusilla Fey, and even Marina was made nervous by her. But Bobby Felix was happy, very happy, perhaps for the first time."

"But why wasn't Pop worried?" I said. "Wasn't anybody trying to stop him?"

"Your father was preoccupied, yes he was. He had other things on his mind," said Sinclair. "Namely you, and your mother. Your birth changed things. Your father became distracted, he withdrew from us, he couldn't see what was coming. *It's just little Bobby Felix*, your father would say. *Nothing to worry about him. Let him have his fun. Glad he found someone for himself. Nothing to fear.*"

Sinclair leaned in close to me, flinching at the fire.

"You will find, child," he said, "that your father was wrong. He was wrong about so many things. We were thieves, we were hustlers all of us, but we had a code, a sense of honor. Only Bobby Felix did not care for rules. Bobby Felix had no code, and on that your father did not reckon. So much magic surrounding Bobby Felix, the strings of fate strumming a song only he could decipher. We should have stopped him, for we did not hate Bobby Felix, no, not at all. Loved him, we loved Bobby Felix, every last one of us. Loved him wrong, we did, but yes, we loved him, in our own way."

"I . . . I understand that," said Tally. "I know just what that means."

"He was our brother," said Sinclair. "And we failed him. And your father, child, your father failed us all."

"But how?" I said. "Is that why Mom left Pop? Is that why we had to flee the swamp?"

Sinclair looked at me, eyes black and sad, just an opal shimmer in the darkness.

"To answer that, we must come to the last night, the hexed night, and I am loath to tell it. It was five years back, and it became apparent that Bobby Felix could no longer be ignored. Your father called us to a secret meeting, because as much as we were all friends, there wasn't any doubt he was our leader. He couldn't help himself but to lead, do you understand? We all had our part."

I did understand. I understood that all too well. I'd been following Pop's lead my whole life.

"The lanterns in our secret room went dark, the candles

whisked out. Magic was afoot, fearsome dreadful magic. The door swung open and there stood Bobby Felix, much changed. Behind him walked Drusilla Fey, chanting a hex, and Marina was pinned against the wall. Bobby Felix had two lackeys with him, two hangers-on that we wouldn't let near us, so vile they were, Cecily Bob and Mr. Hugo. They followed Drusilla Fey, and they were armed. Cecily Bob held his knife to me and Mr. Hugo grabbed your mother. Your father was free, but what could he do with a knife at his wife's throat?"

I couldn't believe it, someone threatening my mom like that. It made me so mad I wanted blood. How could Pop's friend do something like that?

"So what happened?" I said.

"Boss Authority—for that's what Bobby Felix would now be called—challenged your father to a Parsnit duel."

"And Pop whooped him square and good, right?"

"No, child," said Sinclair. "You are much mistaken. Your father lost. And in losing, he doomed us all." Sinclair twitched, his neck muscles flared, his head flinched backward. "Look at me. Look at what I've become. Look at what your father made me."

Sinclair let out a scream and fell down onto the cave floor. He covered his face with his hands and cowered back from the torchlight.

"You must leave," he moaned. "Please. Cecily Bob and

Mr. Hugo are gone now, and you can hide in the trees until you are safe. But you must leave this place, now."

"Why?" I said. "I still don't know what happened."

"Blood has been spilled in this swamp," he said. "There lies a new body for me."

"Is it Pop's?" I said. "Is Pop okay?"

"Make for Baudelaire Quatro's Place," said Sinclair. "That's where your father's headed, I wager. He should go straight to Marina's, but he won't, no matter who counsels him. He wouldn't listen even if I told him, not even if it was old Sinclair. You will learn, child, that your father never listens."

"But is it Pop's blood that got spilled? Is Pop all right?"

Sinclair gnashed his teeth at us, snapping like a dog, his body twitching all over.

"There are bodies gathering," he said. "A feast for the vultures, a feast for me, a feast. The water trickles red. There will be skulls, yes, skulls and leg bones for my collection."

"Please just tell me this," I said. "I know Pop lost, but what did he wager?"

"Swim through the pool at the mouth of the cave." Sinclair's voice went deep, low, and ugly. "Take a deep breath, mind you children, and swim with all your might." Sinclair growled at me. In the darkness his eyes glowed red. "Hurry! Hurry! Before I grow too hungry. Before I can't stop myself."

I felt Tally's furry palm on my arm. "Let's go, Buddy."

Me and Tally made it to the pool where we first got drug

in. Tally dove first and I followed. I swam and I swam until I could see a little flicker of light up ahead. That was it, the sunshine, the sky. It had to be morning by now, I could see the surface of the water, I was almost there. And then something caught my ankle.

It was a vine maybe, some branch of a long-sunk tree snagged right on my trousers. I kicked as hard as I could, but I couldn't break free.

My lungs were burning, and my muscles ached and I was swimming with all my might, but it wasn't doing a lick of good. That daylight was so close I could almost feel it, I could almost feel the sun beating down on my wet skin. But I wasn't ever gonna get there, no sir.

The simple fact of it was I was drowning. Let me tell you, the first thing that surprises you about drowning is how easy it would be to give up, how much your body just wants to shut down and let it go, how easy it can feel to drift down to the bottom and die, right then and there, how you start to want to die, how bad it hurts to hold that air in, how impossibly far away that daylight feels.

I looked up and saw a bug-eyed creature glaring down at me. I nearly screamed, my mouth sucking in water. But no, it was Tally, it was only Tally. She grabbed my hand and tugged and I kicked and my lungs burned and my vision got spotty, and I just about gave up hope. But Tally wasn't going to let me die. Not no way, not no how. That's a true friend for you.

That's the kind of friend that only comes around once or twice in your whole lifetime, and that's a fact. Good old Tally gave my arm a yank so hard it ripped me free from whatever had snagged my leg and Tally pulled me up to the surface, to the good old swamp air, to the morning light burning bright and hot right on my noggin, God bless it.

I was always more of a moonlight kid, to tell you the truth. I liked the nighttime better—the cool air, the hoot owls and tree frogs, the starshine and the moon so big and gorgeous above me that I wanted to rear back and howl like a wolf at it. But by golly, sometimes the sunshine is the only thing that'll do the trick. Sometimes you got to remember that if it weren't for the sunshine, the moon would just be a dark dead rock up there, nothing else to it. It's the light, you know. The light is everything.

We were up in the sweaty swamp air, sucking in breaths, tired arms treading water. The skiff was still there, floating around in circles, the hull bouncing soft off some cypress knees. Tally climbed in first, and she helped me in afterward.

"Thanks," I said. "You saved my life. Again."

"I can tell you one thing, I don't ever want to go back down to that cave." She spat into the water. "Buddy boy, you think we can make it a full day without somebody trying to kill us?"

"I doubt it," I said.

"You and me both."

We curled up in that boat, the both of us wet and exhausted, the bright hot sun pouring through the trees and warming our bodies. We were hidden in the entrance to the Creepy's cave, safe there I knew, even if old Sinclair was scary, even if he'd gone through something more horrible than I could imagine. Truth be told, I hated what he'd said to me about Pop, about how Pop was wrong about things, how he never told the truth. That somehow Pop had doomed him, had doomed the whole swamp. What was I supposed to think about that? How was I supposed to feel about my long-lost pop, my hero, the person I loved most in the world? But I loved what he said about Mom, that she was a witch. Was that what she was doing, up late at night in her kitchen? Was she conjuring things? I knew why she kept quiet about it in general—most towns, even dinky places like Collardsville, aren't safe for witches—but why hadn't she told me? My brain was tired and it was too much for me to think about. The sun warming me, the call of birds off hunting for grub. The whole thing made me tired, it did.

There wasn't any time to sleep though, not yet. We still had my pop to find. We still had to hunt out a cure for Tally.

"Come on," I said, taking up the oars. "We're off for Baudelaire Quatro's Place."

"At least the day's nice," said Tally. A dragonfly circled her head twice and buzzed off. "At least we don't have to do all our searching in darkness, like usual."

Then came the rumble.

Behind us, coming up from the east, was the crackle and groan of black storm clouds creeping up on us. Lightning flickered in the far-off distance. Far-off, but not that far, and galloping mighty and mean toward us.

"Man," said Tally.

"Yep," I said.

I rowed faster.

13

IT ONLY TOOK AN HOUR or so to find Baudelaire Quatro's Place. We saw the top of it looming over the trees and made a beeline straight there. Well, as much of a beeline as a fella can make in a swamp.

When we first saw it I thought my brain had gone buggy. I don't know what I expected, but it sure wasn't this. The trees gave way to an open space about a quarter of a mile wide, where the water was deeper and there wasn't a sandbar in sight. Set deep back in this kind of swamp lagoon, Baudelaire Quatro's Place was a giant wooden building, about eighty feet tall, shaped perfect like a bald human head. I mean that. There were ears on it and everything, even a slightly bent nose, like it had somehow gotten broken in a fight. The eyes were two windows of blue stained glass that seemed lit from inside, and there were double doors right where the mouth would be, and a gaping mouth it was. The head was laid out on a sort of bobbing boardwalk or pier around it, like it had been cut off and was sitting on a plate. It was a floating island of a head that looked like it could rise with the floodwaters and land on soft mud just fine during a drought. It seemed built to survive everything, like the world could end altogether and no one there would hardly notice.

"I heard legends about this place," said Tally, "but I never really believed it was real."

"No kidding," I said.

I didn't know how the thing floated—if it was magic, or just designed all smart by some wacky boat genius—but there it stood, a huge buoy bobbing a little out in the water. A fleet of small boats were tied to a kind of low-lying pier portion, all drifting and bumping into each other a little. Slim canoes and patched-looking dinghies banged into rich folks' yachts, swamp-useless but drifting awful pretty out there. It was clear Baudelaire Quatro's was for folks of all types—provided they could play Parsnit, of course.

"Shoot, Buddy, I don't know about this," said Tally.

The storm was still a little ways off yet, growling and rumbling, warning us that it was headed this way.

"I think maybe we got to try it," I said. "It's the last Parsnit house that doesn't belong to Boss Authority, right? We'll be safe there. Besides, there's a witch for every Parsnit duel. Somebody's bound to be able to help you out."

Tally sighed. "Well, let's get if we're getting."

I rowed us over to the head, where the entrance was, and Tally roped us to the deck. We climbed a little ladder to a sort of boardwalk. Two big wooden doors stood shut tight, right where the wide-open mouth was, and nobody sat watch. That was odd, it sure was, but what could me or Tally do about it?

"You in there, Pop?" I asked the head.

Nobody answered.

I took a deep breath and grabbed the iron door handle and pulled with all my might. The door opened into a small room, a kind of reception area, like maybe what you'd see at an inn. Tally whistled. This place was *nice*. I mean it had a thick red carpet for my muddy old feet and a chandelier full of crystals dangling down over our heads, casting the room and its bright blue wallpaper with sparkles. It was easily the fanciest place I'd ever been in my life. A tiny man stood behind a counter, his back to a door-sized vault, big and metal like at a bank. He wore a black suit and had thin white hair. He was bent over some notebooks scribbling away with a big feather quill. There was a door on the right side of the room and a chair for sitting. A wooden placard on the desk said "Concierge."

"Can I help you?" said the scribbling man, not bothering to look up at us.

"We're looking for someone," I said.

"And you think this 'someone' is currently on the premises of Baudelaire Quatro's Place, is that correct?"

"Yes sir," I said.

"It is not company policy to bandy about the identity of any of our guests, no matter who they be or where they came from or what they may or may not have done. Is that clear?"

"You got a guest book?" I said.

"Of course we have a guest book," he said.

"Can I see it?"

The concierge looked up at us, the light turning his glasses into little silver coins.

"No," he said.

He went back to scribbling.

That made me mad.

I said, "Now listen here—"

The concierge lurched his chest over the counter, until we were eye to eye.

"No, you listen," said the concierge. "I will not have the sacred halls of Baudelaire Quatro's Place sullied by the likes of a couple of mouthy little tramps that just so happened to drift downriver. I detect in your manner a deep lack of respect, both for myself and for the esteemed Mr. Quatro, and I will have no disrespect on these grounds."

"Is that so?" I said.

"Indeed, child, that is so!" said the concierge. "In fact, I ought to bend you over my knee and spank you for speaking to me in such a way. I ought to grab you by the hair and chuck you out the front door and let the gators have their way with you. I ought to do any such thing than sit behind this counter and endure your insolence, but that is what I choose to do, and you may commence thanking whatever higher power you believe in that I don't slit you stomach to gullet and feed your entrails to the nutria. How does that sound?"

He dipped his big feather quill in the inkbottle and got back to it.

"Actually, mister," said Tally, "we come to play."

She whispered to me, "*Show him the cards.*"

I took Pop's cards out of the knapsack and dropped them on the desk.

The concierge stopped his writing for a second. He picked up the cards and unwrapped them carefully. He shuffled them back and forth a few times so fast it looked like he was playing an accordion, same as how I'd seen Pop do it. He flipped over Bright Candle Burning and dragged a long hooked fingernail across it.

Then he sniffed his finger.

His face brightened immediately, and he smiled so big I

thought his cheeks would split. He had a heck of a gleaming row of teeth, this concierge sure did.

"Well why didn't you say so?" He handed the cards back to me. "And you are?"

"I'm Tally," she said, "and this here's Buddy. He'll be the one actually playing the game."

"Buddy and Tally," said the concierge, scribbling in his notebook. "There are currently no duelists seeking challenge," he said, "but you are welcome to wait in the fourth-floor lounge until one should arrive. Though, as according to house rules, if you are challenged, you must of course accept. Until then, you may have use of the facilities." The concierge looked me up and down then, from my mud-splattered boots to my ripped shirt. He cocked a cold eye at me. "I need not tell you to mind yourselves, do I?"

That made me right mad, it did. Just because a fella's had a hard time don't mean he can't conduct himself like a good and proper gentleman. I was about to tell this concierge to learn himself some manners good and quick before he wound up with a split lip and an aching noggin, but Tally cut me off before I could get started.

"Rest assured," said Tally, "you don't need to tell us a durn thing."

"What's behind that door?" I said, pointing toward the vault.

"Nothing that you shall ever see," he said.

"Well you ain't got to be rude about it," I said. "I got an inquiring mind. My mom says that's a noble faculty."

"Perhaps it is," said the concierge, "in little schoolchildren who need their diapers changed."

I said, "Now hold up a minute—"

"If I consent to let you into this establishment," said the concierge, "then you consent to act like a grown-up. Not some ankle-biting snot-nosed little roughneck who belongs in a boys' home for delinquents."

"Thank you," said Tally. "We'll behave, and treat this house with due respect."

"Very well," said the concierge. He turned to me. "You're lucky to have her, you know that, boy?"

I tell you, I was about to say a few words to wipe that smirk right off his face. Tally pinched my arm. Hard. I almost yipped right there in the lobby.

"He knows it," said Tally. "Thank you kindly."

The concierge gestured to the door on the right. It opened by itself to reveal a long, twisty staircase that wove around the whole head, a red carpet laid down, doors every so often, like a hotel. We made our way out of the lobby and up the staircase. The door slammed shut behind us. I was cooling down about then. Man, if Tally hadn't been there I probably would have mouthed off and got us tossed right out of this place. I might have messed everything up, same as me and my no-good hexed-blood luck always did.

"What would I do without you, Tally?" I said.

"You'd probably still be bundled up with that magician, a knife to your throat," she said.

"Good point," I said.

We made our way up the stairs, peeking in each open door, a Parsnit duel happening behind every one. It was hard not to stop and watch.

In one room was an old woman, wrinkled and hunched and stuffed-looking, like a fluffy toy grandma. She sat there with her eyes closed mostly. She didn't even need to look at the cards. She just brushed her fingers over the backs of them and smiled, turning the card she wanted. On a stool next to her sat a girl about my age. She was tiny and pale and blond and could have been the old lady stumbled back in time, so identical they were. She was so short her feet didn't touch the ground, they just kicked and dangled like a restless toddler's. It looked like they were playing as a team, something I'd never seen happen before in a Parsnit duel. But Parsnit could be tricky like that, I guessed, and if it was okay with Baudelaire Quatro, then it was okay with me.

Their opponent was some sweaty-looking fella with bushy hair and a twitch to his lip. He looked like he'd been awake for three days straight, like he could use a shower or two as well. The sitting witch was a bald man with sharp eyebrows whose fingers never quit moving. It was like he

was conducting some invisible magic orchestra, like he con-
jured every whirring syllable into the lantern-bright air. His
eyes were dull and stone gray and I felt cold in his presence,
like he had lived a long time and seen too much and my soul
would shiver at the telling of it all.

The old lady smiled and flipped another card. The Old
Crumbly Castle, that's the card she turned. Now it was time
for the old lady to Orate. The girl next to her went stiff and
rigid, her eyes gone a pupil-less glassy white. Her arms hung
limp down at her sides, and as the old lady's lips began to
move, the girl's did too. It was like a ventriloquist dummy,
you ever seen one of those? The old lady's words belted out
through the sticky-sweet girl voice, a long weird tale of being
a fair maiden trapped in a rotting old castle with no doors
and no windows and no way out. Just a window she could
peek out from and watch the world change.

"And the maiden was a hostage," the doll girl said sweetly.
"A hostage to her body, which was small and frail, and a hostage to her land. The only window in the castle was in her
mind, and that window was great and wide and through it
she could see everything."

I realized she was talking about herself, the old lady was,
about having a bright springtime soul latched to a rusty old
barge of a body. Or maybe she was talking about her granddaughter, or whoever the girl was, forced always to be a
durn bullhorn for a frail old whispering woman. Or else she

meant something else altogether, some big question floating over all our heads, like what's a soul and what's a spirit, and what makes the candle snuff out behind our eyes when we die? She could have been saying any of those things, or all of those things, or even none of them. That was her power, this old lady Orator and her flesh-and-blood dummy.

It was working too, as the poor fella playing opposite her was staring goggle-eyed at the act, his jaw gone slack, looking with a sort of stammering terror like he was toast and he already knew it.

"Come on," said Tally. "Your daddy ain't here."

We passed room after room of Parsnit players deep in concentration, a witch glowering over each table. I never before realized what a collaboration Parsnit is, like it ain't just the two players dueling, but it's also the witch making the story come alive too, so that it's all three of them working together to tell the same story. I passed a fella losing bad to a woman in an ascot and cowboy boots. Her story was the only thing happening in that game, and the best the fella could do was dot the scenery here and there. He just couldn't make his character matter, and that's the truth of it. The presiding witch seemed to agree with me, as she let a tiny twitch of a smile show in the corner of her lips, like it was fun to watch this massacre, like she could see straight into his heart and knew he deserved every bit of what was coming to him.

That thought scared me, if you want to know the truth of it. It scared me plenty.

In one room I saw the lawyer from Gentlesburg. I couldn't believe he'd made it all the way out here, same as I had. He was calm and in his suit, same as before, like he'd just come back from some rich guy board meeting or something. His opponent was a real pretty woman with black hair and a tall top hat with a feather in it. She had a fiddle at the ready. They were about eight cards into the game. It seemed as if they had been dueling for hours and hours.

The woman turned Fire in the Sky and sat rigid and upright. She brought her fiddle to her neck and let it rip, playing a sad low melancholy song, something bright and burning in the night, something far off and lovely, something you felt couldn't last. It was so beautiful I almost burst into tears right then. Tally grabbed my hand and we stood there in the doorway, listening. All of a sudden the lawyer came in singing a harmony, his voice high and pure, not an ounce of grit to it, and together they sang the song of the high far-off burning thing, a star maybe, that was falling fast and low, already doomed. When they finished both the woman and the lawyer laid their heads on the table and wept, and the witch stretched her plump hands out to each of them, as if in a blessing.

"I guess that's one you'd call a tie," said Tally.

"Yeah," I said. "They both won that one, and that's the truth of it."

We kept walking until we ran out of rooms. There was only one door left, and that led to the top floor. We opened the door to a big room, right where the head's brain would be. It was some kind of restaurant or lounge. There weren't any windows to the place, so no daylight or starlight or moonlight got in there, just the high gleaming chandeliers and lamps scattered all over, like we were in some kind of cave, like there wasn't any outside world at all. A small band was playing—a banjo and an accordion and a washboard—with a tiny man like a carnival barker hollering over them, doing a funny little dance in wooden shoes. He had on a bowler hat and every time he took it off the air above his head filled with little glittering sparkles. Folks ate, folks drank, folks argued. Waiters in crisp suits zipped around with plates of food. There must have been a hundred people in that upper room, truth be told.

Tally snatched a loaf of bread from a waiter walking by and broke me off a piece. It was hot and soft and reminded me of home, it did, it was just the way Mom would have baked it. That made me sad a little bit, because all of a sudden I missed Mom, I missed our house bakery, I missed even tiny sleepy Collardsville, dump that it was. But now wasn't the time for pitiful thoughts like that, no sir. I was on a mission to find Pop. He was counting on me. There wasn't time yet to miss where I came from.

Over in the far corner sat a bunch of bedraggled folks, so tired they weren't hardly blinking. They just stared off into nothing, their eyes bloodshot and shattered looking.

"What's wrong with those guys?" I said.

"I've heard about this," said Tally. "They got the wore-outs. It's when the magic in Parsnit starts to get too much for folks and they can't leave it alone. They can't eat or sleep or hardly do nothing. They just want another taste of the game, a bit more of that magic working on them from the cards. It's a sad state, it is."

"No kidding," I said. "I never knew Parsnit had a down-side. I mean, apart from witches' bonds and whatever it was that turned Sinclair into the Creepy."

"Magic's always got a consequence," said Tally. "Grand-dad used to tell me that all the time." And she looked sad a minute, like maybe she missed her granddad a little bit, cruel and awful as he was.

"Looking for somebody?" said a portly fella with red cheeks and massive muttonchops.

"Yes sir," I said. "I'm looking for my pop." Tally elbowed me in the side, like *hush your durn mouth*. But what could I do about it? "You don't work for Boss Authority, do you?"

"'Course not," said the man. He crossed himself three

times and spit on the carpet. "And I got a mind to whoop your scrawny little butt for asking me a question like that."

"Sorry," I said. "I just don't want to get my pop in any more trouble. His name's David Josiah Pennington, you ever heard of him?"

The man's eyes went wide and his smile did a little jump. "Your dad is Davey Boy Pennington? Is he here?"

"If I knew the answer to that," I said, "then I wouldn't be looking for him."

"Quite right, quite right," said the man. He thrust his hand out to me. "Name's Radegar Kelly."

"Buddy," I said.

"I'm Tally," said Tally, and Radegar bowed.

"Imagine that," he said "Davey Boy Pennington back in the Swamplands. It might be time for a shakeup here, and let me tell you, that shakeup is rightly due. Boss Authority has ruined this swamp, he has. We are standing in the last free house left."

"Sorry," said Tally, "but those folks over there don't look too free." She pointed at the half-dead men, sitting there all smelly and foul-clothed and glazy-eyed.

"You're right about that," said the man. "Parsnit takes an awful toll on folks who ain't got the proper constitution. Heck, it takes a toll on all of us who play. And yet we do. Peculiar predicament, ain't it?"

"I guess," said Tally. "I tell you right now, this game ain't for me."

"But I reckon it is for this one, ain't it?" he said, pointing at me. "Bet you can't drag this little fella away from a Parsnit table once his number's called. On account of who his daddy is, I mean."

"What are you getting at, mister?" I said.

"What I'm getting at is how about we have us a little duel, you and me?" he said. "I know you got a deck, else they wouldn't have let you past the front room. How about it, son? How about you play ol' Radegar?"

That flat flabbergasted me. I never counted on being actually challenged in Baudelaire Quatro's Place. I didn't figure there'd be anybody who would want to.

"I don't know, mister," I said. "I think I ought to get back to finding Pop. Don't got much time for games right now."

"But this ain't any mere game, son," said Radegar. "It's Parsnit. Knowing him, your pop will keep just fine, wherever he is."

"It ain't right," I said. "I got to go."

A voice spoke up behind me.

"In point of fact, Master Pennington, you may *not* go."

The concierge was standing right there behind me in his little suit.

"What have you got to do with anything?" I said. "I'm leaving. I got to find my pop."

"I have everything to do with everything," said the concierge, "and I say to you, if you are offered a duel, you must accept. Those are Mr. Baudelaire Quatro's House Rules."

"Thank you, Mr. Concierge," said Radegar, bowing a little. "I was afraid this little scamp was gonna try and weasel out of a duel."

"How'd you get up here so fast?" I said.

"Mr. Quatro himself told me," said the concierge. "I was informed that a challenge had been issued."

"Is the old fella around?" said Radegar. "I've been wanting to meet him for ages, him being an original Parsnit player and all. Heard he was quite the Orator in his day, could flat talk you to weeping. Gent must be old now though, huh? Least over a hundred."

"Mr. Quatro is indisposed at the moment," said the concierge.

"Then how did he hear us?" I said.

"This house *is* Mr. Quatro, in a manner of speaking," said the concierge. "Not a word is uttered that he does not hear, and there is not a nook, cranny, or closet in which Mr. Quatro is not somehow present. If you are in his House, in a sense, then you are inside Mr. Quatro's Head as well."

"I don't get it," I said.

"And you don't have to," said the concierge. "The fact remains, a challenge has been issued, and you must accept it."

"But I ain't ever played before," I said. "Not really."

"Well I'll be sure and go easy on you," said Radegar with a wink. "Besides, your daddy being who he is, I'm sure you're a durn natural."

I looked at Tally, and she looked back at me. The heck was I supposed to do?

"Don't worry now," said Radegar. "We won't put nothing up for wager, no witch's bond to keep us true. We'll just play a few rounds and you can see how a real pro does it. Who knows? Maybe I can teach you a few things that your daddy never got around to."

"Fine," I said. "Just a few rounds, not even a full duel. And remember, I ain't never played before."

"That a boy!" shouted Radegar. "Grab me a bottle of something nice and lead us on, Mr. Concierge!"

The concierge took us downstairs, to an empty room on the third floor. Me and Radegar took a seat at either side of the table. Tally stood next to me, looking about as nervous as I'd ever seen her.

"Who's sitting witch?" said Radegar. "It better not be Betty Wettach again. That woman durn hates me, she does. Always gives me the weak magic."

"I'll be presiding." A beautiful silver-haired woman in a long white gown with sequins glimmering in little eyeballs all over her dress walked into the room. "Call me Miss Arabella."

She held her hand out to us. Radegar took it and kissed it. When it was my turn I just gave it a little shake, and the lady laughed, a sparkling high sound like bells.

Radegar clapped his hands twice. "Gather around folks, we're about to play some Parsnit!"

That's when I noticed it wasn't just us in the room anymore. All kinds of folks had crammed into the back, gamblers and duelists and drinkers, the lawyer and the violin woman (who seemed to be holding hands), the stinky folks and the well-dressed, all of them, guests and house regulars and new players who probably only just darkened the doors like us, some even spilling out into the hallway, peeking in on tiptoes—all to watch me, Davey Boy Pennington's son, play his first game of Parsnit.

I gulped.

Tally put her hand on my shoulder and whispered in my ear, "You're attracting an awful lot of attention, considering no one's supposed to know we're here."

"I'm not real sure what I'm supposed to do about it," I whispered back. "I'd be a liar if I said I wasn't scared."

"You'd be a durn fool too," she said. "But you're here, and now you got to play. Do your best not to lose too much in the process."

That's the thing about Parsnit. I know it seems like just a card game, where you play a few hands and tell a story or two and that's that. But the game goes much further. You play and it feels like you're handing a little bit of your soul over too, like it's your heart and guts battling somebody else's hearts and guts. It ain't just the players either. In a truly great Parsnit duel, the audience's hearts beat fierce and wild and all their hair stands on its ends.

It's magic, real honest-to-God magic, that's what I'm telling you.

Radegar tossed me his deck to shuffle and I gave him Pop's. The cards had a weird energy to them, a fishy stink of swamp water and grit. They felt different than Pop's did, made of coarser stuff. I wasn't much good at shuffling, couldn't do anything flashy like Pop, but I got the job done. We traded decks back and laid them on the stone table and it was decided that Radegar, being the one who issued the challenge and all, should draw the first card.

He flipped the Mountebank, first try. Radegar whistled real loud and all the house regulars took to chuckling. You could tell that was the card he wanted, the card he felt his heart most attached to.

But hold up a minute. I took a closer look at his card, and it didn't seem a bit like any of the other Mountebank cards I'd ever seen. Sure the figure was there, a fellow in a top hat and suit, a little seedy-looking, hawking his wares and caught midgesture with a bottle of some sort, probably some miracle cure made out of old bathwater. But instead of being tall and lean with big owl eyes and thin cheeks, the Mountebank on this card was portly, red-faced, with a pair of muttonchops, big and bushy as Radegar's. I remembered something Pop had said about how Parsnit cards bound themselves to a player, how they changed as he changed, how they came to be about him. You could almost hear the sweet lying words come tumbling right out of his mouth, you could feel the little tug of his lies begging you to buy, urging you on, pulling you toward this one little object that might change your life, that could open up worlds to you, that could make your pop love you for real and end all the curses on your blood and get you home safe and sound, that would make your life bearable forever.

Then I snapped out of it. Miss Arabella was smiling, and I knew this was a powerful Parsnit card indeed, truly one tied to Radegar's own heart.

Radegar began to Orate. It went a little like this:

"Now welcome, ladies and gentlemen and other folk, to the most sad and lamentable tale of old Turnjack the Mountebank. A man persecuted beyond all others, pursued by ungrateful associates, hounded by unscrupulous lawyers, and dogged by impecunious masses . . ."

He droned on and on like that. Radegar wasn't much of an Orator, and that was a fact. He could tell a good yarn, but he used too many words, he stumbled over himself, he kept distracting you from the card, from the story, from the heart of the man. That I knew very well. Even Miss Arabella had a hard time keeping track. I could see Turnjack the Mountebank quite well in my mind's eye, I could see him wrangle his wares and argue with his wife, I could feel how wronged he felt by the world, how he felt there was no real place for him, but it didn't break my heart any. Felt a bit to me like Turnjack deserved all he got.

All in all, it wasn't much of an introduction.

It was my turn. I felt real nervous, hoping in my heart that I would draw the Fish Boy, the card I knew the best, the card that I always saw myself in, or better yet, *felt* myself in. It's hard to explain I guess. It's like, have you ever looked at a painting or heard a song or just been somewhere beautiful— maybe an old creaky house or a sunlit field or in front of a wild oak tree, just as the moon was rising—and felt like, yes, this is me, this is me exactly, I could be looking in a mirror of my dreams? Have you ever felt anything like that at all in your life? If not, well, take it from old Buddy here—you ain't been looking hard enough. It's out there for you, the feeling of recognizing yourself in something else, and when you find it, oh it will feel so good deep inside of you. It'll change you forever.

Everyone was silent. I sure hoped I wasn't going to embarrass myself by flipping over a home card, or an action or a word, anything that I couldn't call my person. That sure would be an unrecoverable mistake. That would more or less ensure that I didn't stand a chance in this game, that I'd gone and lost for sure.

The Fish Boy, I prayed. *The Fish Boy please.*

I flipped my card.

There he stood, a little awkward, his face perplexed and determined, same as the way I saw myself every time I looked over the edge of the skiff and into the waters, holding aloft a cup with a weird-eyed fish springing out of it. The Fish Boy. My card. I was so happy right then I could have cried.

The rest of the crowd felt it too. There were a couple of gasps even, some yokels slamming down glasses in disgust and some hollering out in applause. Tally clapped her hands and squeezed my shoulder and that made me feel good, real good, actually. I had done it. I flipped my Person card first try.

Now it was my turn to Orate.

My turn to Orate.

Mine.

I realized right then that I'd never Orated before. Not out loud anyway, not even once. I'd only ever done it in my head. And let me tell you, Orating all alone in your head is much, much different than doing it out loud, much less doing it out loud in front of a bunch of seasoned Parsnit pros in the last free house in the swamp.

I took a deep breath and let it out slow, like I'd seen other Parsnit players do when they were all nervous.

"Well . . . ," I said.

My voice cracked. It *did*. A few of the house folks cackled. Even old Radegar grinned a little bit, though you could tell he was trying to hide it. That made me mad, it did. I wanted to whoop all the smiles right off those fellas' faces.

"Well," I said again, fiercer now, trying to sound as grown-up and manly as possible. "This is a tale about a small-town boy living far away from his home. Far, far from the land of his birth, the Riverlands, where the water is always rushing and the boats are on the move and the source of all your food is right there, just outside your door, a whole river of fortune, a treasure chest you drop a line in and pull up who knows what. This is the story of a small-town boy exiled from his beloved pop, forced to coop up with his mom in a land of dirt and gossip and boredom. This is a story about a boy who loved his pop so much he'd do anything to find him back, who would face any kind of dangers, who would stare down death in his one single black beady eye just to gain back what he'd lost, his pop and his river life, every last thing he'd ever held dear."

I said it just like that, with my voice deeper and fuller and stronger than I knew possible. I said it all and I didn't crack even once, and that was a fact. It was the story of my life as I saw it, and I told it as true and direct as I could.

It didn't quite seem to do the trick though. I could tell the crowd heard it, that they could see it too, even old Radegar's eyes were wide and focused as the pictures flickered in his mind. They heard it, they even saw it, but it didn't crack them open, not one bit. My story didn't make it into their hearts.

I wondered why.

Still, I hadn't fallen flat on my face, and that was a fact. I could do this. I could play Parsnit as well as anybody else, and I had my first round to prove it.

Next came the Home card. Radegar drew his three, and his eyes went wide with big obvious pleasure, like he'd pulled exactly the cards he wanted. He laid down the Wayward River, one of my favorite cards, and one of Pop's too. You could recognize it, the way the water curved and curled, how rocks jutted out of the blue like the river's own fangs, like if you didn't keep rushing by the river would snap its jaws shut and swallow you whole. The Wayward River is the card for bandits and wild folks, for those who live by the cunning of their minds and their skill with a knife, the exact kind of folk my pop was.

But again, Radegar's card looked a little bit different from Pop's. It was the Wayward River, sure, except instead of the swirling gray-blue gone on and on, it was the murky green of the swamp, the water rushing by in a slow and steady current, tugging quiet underneath. Instead of rocks jabbing upward like in Pop's deck, Radegar's had knotty cypress knees poking out, with gray moss beards dangling down to the water, and in the far background of the card, a great long distance away, there was a figure holding a lantern, standing upright in his boat like he was searching for something long gone and lost. It was a beautiful card when Radegar drew it, just as free and wild as Pop's, but with a mournful side, like all those good times came at a price.

And that was the story Radegar told. How the wild Mountebank floated downriver on his boat, selling cures that were certain to work, absolutely certain, if only applied right and in the proper dosage, though nobody ever bothered to do that. How he was welcomed into homes all over the bayou, and how he welcomed himself into homes when nobody else was there. Never to steal nothing, mind you, but to sleep in a real bed, with covers and a top sheet, under an old quilt someone's beloved grandma had sewn. To sit at a chair and drink a cup of water, pretending that it was his chair and his cup of water, that he had a loving wife to draw it for him, that his boy came to sit in his lap, grateful he was home. The Mountebank was just lonely, he was, out on the wild waters looking for love, for family, for a place to call home. It was a sad place, the Mountebank's Wayward River, where every bit of freedom just made him wish to be tied down by something good, something permanent, some kind of home.

What a load of hogwash.

But it seemed to connect with a lot of the Parsnit regulars. I mean that. Wasn't nearly a dry eye in the entire room. Old men in ratty clothes shook their heads sadly, the lines grew on sad ladies' smiles. Everyone seemed older and more alone, like all this rambling and card playing wore on a body. Some of the oldest and most bedraggled folks even clapped. That kind of junk made me mad. Who didn't love the Wayward River? Of course it isn't a real house-and-a-yard home, that's the whole point. Who in the world gets all the freedom they want and winds up whining about having it? A durn fool, that's who. I was about ready to stomp Radegar and his pitiful woe-is-me Orating into the dirt, if you wanted to know the truth about it.

My turn was up, and I was ready.

Please give me the Bramble, or the Long Way Round. Heck, give me the durn Cold Dark City. I been there. I could make a story out of it.

I took a deep breath and drew my three cards.

It was a disaster. I drew the Moanful Ghost, the Dolly Witch, and the Corpse Laugher. Not a single one of those was a Home card.

I lost. I lost already. My deck blew it for me. I didn't even get a chance to try.

I just sat there, my face gone blank, staring at the three dead cards in my hand.

"Go on, boy," said Radegar. "Play your card."

I laid them all faceup. The whole room erupted in laughter. I had lost, and lost spectacularly. Only the worst Parsnit players—the ones who don't know their decks, the ones with not a lick of magic in them, the ones with hexed durn blood—don't draw a single Home card when it's time. I'd shamed myself and shamed the deck and shamed Pop too. My head hung so heavy I couldn't bear to lift it and look a single Parsnit player in the eye.

"Well," said Radegar, looking anywhere but right at my face, "not bad for your first try, I suppose. It ain't like Parsnit runs in the blood. Not like luck, anyhow. Who knows? Maybe your daddy ain't all he's cracked up to be either. He whooped me solid when we first met, but that might have been a fluke. Regardless, it was nice to Orate a little bit. It was nice to see my words float up and become something, you know what I mean?"

I packed up my cards and put them back in the knapsack. I was so ashamed I could hardly bear it. Tally gave me a little pat on the back, like *nice try*, and that somehow made me feel even worse.

"Sorry," I said. "I guess I messed it up pretty bad, huh?"

"Everyone's got a first duel," said Radegar. "Put her there."

He reached his hand across the table and I shook it, even if his palm was hot and clammy. The Parsnit players all clapped. It was the end of the duel, and I'd blown it royally. I only hoped Pop wouldn't hear of it, wherever he was.

Slowly everyone filed out of the room except for Miss Arabella. She walked over to me and Tally and sat beside us. She put her hand on my neck and it felt soft and cool, like a breeze on the hottest summer day. It put me at ease a little bit.

"Can I tell you a secret?" she said.

"Yeah, I guess," I said. "Though secrets ain't been a whole lot of help to me lately."

"Would you like to know what Parsnit cards really do?" she said. "Why witches make them?"

"I sure would," said Tally. "I been wondering that my whole life."

"Parsnit is much older than this game here," she said. "The cards are, anyway. They were made by witches and artists—who frankly aren't all that different, if you want to know the truth about it—ages and ages ago. They were a means of telling a story."

"Not to be rude," I said, "but that ain't hardly a secret. Everybody knows that. And witches gave the Parsnit cards to regular folks so they could have a taste of magic themselves, right?"

"It also gives witches a way to make money," said Tally. "Err, not that you would need that."

"All true, yes," said Miss Arabella. "But that isn't the point. These cards show people and places, images and symbols. They're the stuff of dreams. So often a Parsnit player will use the cards to tell a story that's really just her own story as she best sees it. She'll tell the story of her dreams. It's her own legend she's spinning. Take care to remember that each legend is just one person's truth in a whole bunch of other truths that whirl and swirl around each other. Sometimes the truths agree, and other times they don't. Be careful not to take one single person's truth as the final say in the matter."

"You saying Parsnit cards lie?" I said.

"I'm warning you not to use the cards to lie to yourself, Buddy," she said.

"Miss Arabella," said Tally. "Can I ask you for a favor?"

"Sure, honey," she said. "Go right on ahead."

Tally was looking right bashful, her face down to the floor, wiggling her foot back and forth like she was grinding out a tiny fire.

"You seem like a real powerful witch," she said, "and I got this problem, with how I was born."

"You mean with how you were born, being spider-folk and all?"

"You could tell?" said Tally.

"I wouldn't be much of a witch if I couldn't," said Miss Arabella. "But it's a great gift, being spider-folk. Many would kill—and I mean that literally—to have an ounce of your power."

"But I don't want it," said Tally. "I've never wanted it. I hate it. I hate it more than anything in the whole world."

Miss Arabella rubbed her chin all thoughtful-like.

"I suppose I could repress the spider part of you, yes," she said. "I could hide it deep in your mind, waiting there, curled up and asleep for all your life. Would you like that, honey?"

"Yes," said Tally. "I'd like that more than anything."

"It will be a hard spell," said Miss Arabella, "and quite painful. Are you sure you want that part of you hidden?"

Tally looked up at Miss Arabella, her eyes soft and unfierce and tearful. "I don't want to be a monster anymore."

But Miss Arabella wasn't listening. Her face had gone blank, like the moon, like someone had up and wiped it clean.

"What's wrong?" I said.

An explosion sounded on the fourth floor. Folks were screaming.

Through the open doorway I saw a woman dressed in a wedding gown that stretched long and elegant twelve feet behind her like a train of white ghosts running down the hallway, her head thrown back cackling, her eyes red as fire. She had to be a witch, I just knew it. Her hair was black and flowing behind her, her teeth were jagged like fangs, and her fingernails grew out long in front of her like knives.

Miss Arabella whirled toward the door, and her dress seemed to rise and cover both me and Tally, making us small somehow, sweeping us right under her skirts to where we clung to her legs all old and thin and bony.

"Drusilla Fey, honey, is that you?" said Miss Arabella.

"Arabella," said the other lady. "Looking well, considering."

"I am under a bit of duress at the moment," said Miss Arabella. I could feel her legs quaking, I could feel how brave and afraid she was.

"There's no resistance now, dear," said Drusilla Fey. "Bow to him, and he will show you mercy."

"I think not, honey," said Miss Arabella. "I don't consider myself one to bow to any living person, and not to borrowed magic such as his."

"Oh but you *will* bow," said Drusilla Fey, "even if he has to break your legs to make you do it."

"If you have come here to take my life, Drusilla Fey, then I suggest you get it over with, and quickly. I am not one for delaying the inevitable."

"That would be too easy now, wouldn't it?" said Drusilla Fey. "I look forward to watching you grovel at my feet."

I heard what sounded like a stampede down the hall, folks screaming and hollering war shrieks, Parsnit players fleeing and Boss Authority's men hunting them down.

"Ta-ta, Arabella," said Drusilla Fey. "Don't forget, I gave you a chance."

And then she was gone. I don't know how I knew it, but it was true. It was like I could feel her leave, she was so powerful the air couldn't relax until she left the room. Miss

Arabella swept her dress back and we were sitting on our stools again. I don't know how she did it, except for magic.

"Thank you," I said.

"We were lucky," she said. "Come quickly, children."

Miss Arabella grabbed my hand and I grabbed Tally's and we took off running down the stairs of the head, past the eyes and the little nook of the nose and around the earlobes until we were at the bottom, the wide-open mouth, the concierge's front desk. Miss Arabella stopped right where she was and yanked my hand tight. It was like a current was zapped through us, and both me and Tally were frozen stiff right on the spot. I couldn't hardly have flapped my eyelids if I wanted.

The concierge's desk had been flipped over, tossed on its side, and where the secret door had been now stood a huge hole in the wall. The concierge stood in the back of the room, holding something in a big glass jar.

And in front of him stood a short, squat man with a back slightly hunched, his arms thick with hair and tattoos, his right hand squiggled all over in symbols that looked obscure and magic, his left hand a giant chunk of metal. A pony-tail that swished back and forth on its own like a dog's tail dangled down his back. I knew him, somehow, I knew him in my heart, I knew him from stories told. There he stood before me.

Boss Authority.

"You shall not have him," said the concierge. "It is neither fair nor good. In fact, it is exceedingly indecent. No, I simply will not allow it."

"Little fella," said Boss Authority. "I don't think you got much choice in the matter." He took two steps toward the man, the buckles on his boots going *clink clank* with every step. "Come on, now. Let me see him." Boss Authority held out that iron hand. The pointer finger whisked a *here, here* movement. "Let me see what's left of old Baudelaire Quatro."

It was like you see with magic magnets sometimes, the way they pull metal toward them. The glass jar began to draw slowly toward Boss Authority. You could tell the concierge was mystified, fighting it as best he could, but he could not hold his arms back.

I saw what was in the jar. It was a man's head, shaved bald and beardless, with a slightly hooked nose and bright beaming blue eyes. It was the exact head of the building we were in. It was Baudelaire Quatro's head. The eyes blinked twice, and the mouth stretched open in horror. The head in the jar was very much alive, it was. The head in the jar was screaming for its dear life.

I felt Miss Arabella's hand tense up and I heard the slightest whisper escape her lips. She was doing magic. The concierge's eyes blinked aware and he yanked the head in the jar back to himself. He set it down on the ground and squatted himself down, rolled his sleeves up, and lifted his dukes. He was ready for a fight.

Boss Authority whirled around. Miss Arabella's hand went ice-cold. Boss Authority's left eye was deep brown and rimmed with yellow and orange, his right eye a blank white swirl. His nose was knobby and cruel, his face a mask of scars and tattoos and magic carvings into his skin. He had a weeping lady tattooed on his cheek, washing her hair in her own tears, and an hourglass on his neck with all the sand in the top part, none dripping down, like time would never run out on him, not ever.

He saw me. Boss Authority saw me, and it was like I could hear his voice whispering in my ears, I could feel him in the thud of my heart. Boss Authority knew me, he knew just who I was. He could hear the very thoughts jumbling around in my head. Boss Authority knew I was Davey Boy's son.

I thought he would come for me then. I thought he would walk *clink clank* across the floor and grab me by my cheeks and snap my neck right then and there.

But the concierge was changing. His arms got plumper and his belly dropped and his hands went clawlike and his nose became a snout, two big tusks jolting out from under his lip. He hunkered down, a great warthog beast on all fours in the hall, growling in fury.

Boss Authority whipped back around. "All right little

fella," he said to the concierge, and spat on the fine red carpet. "Have it your way."

Above us we heard Drusilla Fey's cackling and the screams of folks as they tumbled down the staircase. Miss Arabella yanked my hand and we were running then, out the front door mouth past Boss Authority's men and onto the pier. Rain beat down hard on us, lightning ripping glowing gashes in the gray clouds. Baudelaire Quatro's Place was a wreck. The giant wooden head was on fire at the top, flames leaping high like some kind of hellish crown, and someone had busted both eyes out. Folks were leaping out of holes in the cheeks, not even bothering to untie their boats, just swimming off into the swamp for dear life. Boss Authority's men were after them, low-down pirate-looking folks all scraggly and desperate, nothing but hate and glee in their eyes. Something had changed in the swamp, it had. Boss Authority was out for blood.

Miss Arabella followed us to our skiff. We untied it and hopped inside. Already rainwater was filling it up at the bottom, and I got busy bailing with my hands. Tally looked up at Miss Arabella, standing there on the dock.

"So can you help me?" said Tally. "Please."

"I'm sorry, honey," she said. "There isn't any time. It would take me many days to prepare a cure, and I fear there aren't many days left for me if I linger here any longer."

"But where are you going?" said Tally.

Miss Arabella's face was long and worn and thin, grief stretching her skin so tight it could have been a mask.

"Far, far away, to the deep north forests. I'll be safe there. Goodbye, children. Follow the narrow path, right through those trees over there, and don't you dare turn off to the right or left. Your skiff's small enough to squeeze through, and if Boss Authority's chasing anybody, it'll be the big boats. Make for Marina's Place, if you can. She'll give you refuge."

"Please," said Tally. "Can't you do anything for me?"

"If I'm able, I'll return and bring you a hex, honey. That I promise." She nodded to me. "And good luck finding your daddy."

Miss Arabella stepped off the boat and onto the wind-lashed water, walking the same as if it were dry land. Rain pelted down on all of us but it just seemed to miss her entirely, like she wasn't touched by it. Miss Arabella walked into the trees and vanished. I knew right then that neither me nor Tally would ever see her again.

Tally was heartbroken, I could tell, and I wanted to comfort her, I wanted to throw my arms around her and hug her and tell her that it would be okay, that I thought she was great just the way she was, that we'd work this out somehow, together. But then I heard Drusilla Fey's cackle ripple across the water and I heard the screams of the Parsnit folk and I knew there wasn't time for comfort, not now, not yet.

So I rowed fast as I could away from the lagoon through the path, between two twirling cypresses and back into the wild tangled darkness of the swamp.

14

SOMEHOW WE GOT AWAY. I figured Miss
Arabella cast a hex on our boat, because a big fog rose up
around us, like we were traveling in a cloud. But I knew
folks were after us, they were, Boss Authority's men. We
were right to float the narrow path through the waters,
the one Miss Arabella bid us take. The rain lashed at us
in cold prickles. Here and there we saw flickers, lanterns
and torches burning through the darkness, lighting the air
through the trees and tangle vines and rain. We heard hollers, men screeching commands at one another, cackling
out like demons. The hunt was on, Boss Authority was making his move. I only hoped Pop was okay, wherever he was.
I hoped Pop was hunting us too.

That made me wonder though. Why hadn't Pop found

me yet? Didn't he know I was out looking for him?

The skinny path through the trees had widened now, but it was still boatless except for us, everyone else escaped down other ways. We were lost and afraid. A giant cypress keeled over not ten feet from us, just like God himself had given it a yank, its roots writhing up out of the swamp water like some tentacled horror beast come slithering up to swallow us. I was scared. I thought we were gonna die.

A bright high sound cut through the storm, lovely and silvery amid the thunder rumbles, like it was the sound of the moon and stars themselves coming out.

"What's that?" I said.

"Hush," said Tally.

It was singing, a man's voice calling out a hymn of mourning. It spooked me, drifting out in the rain and storm like that. An old building loomed ahead of us, crooked-roofed and half-sunk in the muck. It had a tall spire on the top in a cross shape. The windows that weren't busted were multicolored, and candlelight shone out from them in strange warbles. The singing was coming from inside, an old sweet song, sad as could be. You could just barely make it out over the rain and wind and thunder.

"Is that a church?" said Tally.

"I think so. But who would build a church this far down in the swamp?"

"Bunch of crazy folks," said Tally. "We ought to keep going. We ought not to stop here."

We rowed by the church, the rain battering our boat, water rising in inches on the bottom. I stopped a second, shielding my eyes from the rain. I wanted a good look at it. I wanted to see inside. The church was burnt, yes, and the walls had been blackened and crumbled, and the whole thing looked like it could fall in on itself at any moment. But something seemed familiar about it to me, a memory long blurred and faded, just a scrap left in my mind. I had seen this church before.

I peered inside and saw an old man in priest robes singing, banging away on a warped piano. He was bald with a long gray beard down to his chest. A small dog swam down the aisle to the altar with his tongue out. He headed toward the priest, howling along to the song. The priest laughed, bent down, and petted the dog. He seemed to be crying, the priest did, and he went back to singing loud and sweet and sad, of strength in the trying times, of the happiness of the days to come. I guess I mean that he was singing about hope, which is maybe the best and saddest thing of all.

I don't know, it got to me.

"Are you okay?" hollered Tally over the wind and rain. "You look like you're gonna be sick."

The priest looked up and saw us. He hopped off the

piano bench and scrambled down the aisle, water up past his knees. He leaned out the door of the half-sunk church and called to us.

"Ahoy!" he said. "Two strays out in the rain. You're two little kitties got lost, ain't ye?"

His eyes were wide and loony in the lightning-light. His grin was too wide, his teeth crooked and awkward. This wasn't right. We needed to leave, and now.

"Folks after you?" he said. "I seen their fires, I seen their lights. Looking for you, aren't they? Who else would they be looking for except two little stray kittens lost out in the rain?"

"I ain't any kitten," I said.

"Me neither," said Tally.

"Hmm," said the priest. He rubbed his chin, all thought-ful. "Yes, yes, maybe that's the wrong word. It could be no disgrace to you, of course, though the felines might take offense, truth be told. Nothing stronger than a stray cat, and that's a fact. Nothing scrappier, nothing better at surviving. I've seen snow and rain and hail fall on a litter of kitties, and I've seen them crawl back meowing for food come spring, come summer. I've seen hurricanes blow houses away, but the stray kittens are fine, they're always fine. So if it's the word 'kitten' that's set you against me, well, I would say the mistake is yours, children."

The priest tilted his head all crooked at me, same way a

bird does, and blinked twice. I squinted back at him, the rain battering my face.

"Well, come in out of the rain," he said. "Though the rain does get through this roof indeed, but only in little droplets, sprinkles, like a blessing. A holy blessing, every raindrop is. They have names, they do, each one. God names them, and he knows them, before they splash into the great pool of things and become a part of greater water. Even then he knows their names. Just as he knows yours. Do you know God's name, children?"

"Let's get out of here," whispered Tally. "This guy's nuts."

I nodded at her.

"So long, mister," I said.

But we heard voices then, hollers above the thunder, and on the far side of a thicket of cypresses and dry land came the glow of lanterns. A search party. Out hunting for us.

"Go if you must," said the priest. "Go and I bless you. But know this, kitty-children. There is always refuge for you in the church! Yes, in my church! Where the water rises"—he pointed down to the flood that was long past his knees—"and the love always rains down from above."

He reached his arms out long and wild, the sleeves rolling down over his skinny bare scarred arms, his fingers outstretched, like he was trying to wrap his arms around the whole building.

More hollers from the fog and rain. I didn't know what to do. I was scared to trust this man, this crazy bearded old fella in his burnt-down sunk-down ruined church, but I was more scared of being caught by Boss Authority's men. It didn't feel like there was a right thing to do. Then I remembered something from a conversation Mom and Pop had a long time ago, something about water and love being the two strongest things there were. I guess I'm saying there was something about this priest that I liked.

"Be quick children," said the priest. "Hurry."

We rowed the skiff inside the church and the priest pulled it down the aisle, splashing all the way. He pulled it right to the altar, a tall podium of stone and wood that had a sun and a moon painted on it. "Out, out!" he said. We hopped into the water. Then he pushed the boat through a hole in the back wall of the church. I started to say something but he shushed me with one long finger to his lips. The priest leaned in close and whispered in my ear. "She won't get far. It's all tangles and brambles behind there. It's just the spot for her to hide, don't you worry. Now for the children. Where shall the children be hid?"

He looked up above us, to the church rafters. Moss hung down from them, creeper vines dangled snakelike and there were birds too, a row of mournful brown owls like tiny silent monks gathered together to pray over us.

"Up, up!" said the priest.

The church wall was torn and chinked, with footholds aplenty, so long as you could see them. Tally made short work up to the rafters, her being part spider and a better climber than me besides. I had a tougher time. I kept falling off, splashing myself back in the water. The priest had to stand on a pew and grab me by the waist and boost me up. Tally pulled me the rest of the way. We crouched together on a crossbeam, praying like crazy it wouldn't crack or snap or fall. I was wet and scared, shivering in the swamp heat. But the owls weren't shaking, no sir. The owls looked on at us like they weren't surprised one bit, like they'd been waiting here for us to show up their whole lives. I almost wanted to stick my hand out and introduce myself, see if they'd shake it. But I didn't have time, because right then a skiff approached the doorway to the church, and I heard two familiar awful voices cutting through the rain and wind.

A tall skinny figure hunched over holding a lantern, and a squat thick pumpkin-shaped fella sat next to him. I felt like I knew the both of them well by then, ever since they busted in and wrecked my perfect night with Pop. I never quite seemed to be able to escape them, Cecily Bob and Mr. Hugo. They rowed right up to the church and stepped out into the flooded aisles. Cecily Bob tied the boat to one of the pews while Mr. Hugo peered up at the priest.

"Seen any children pass this way?" asked Mr. Hugo.

"Eh?" said the priest, cupping his ear. "I beg your pardon, sirs, but my hearing's near gone at this point. Could ye speak up a little?"

"Have you seen any children or not?" hollered Mr. Hugo.

"Children? In a night like this?" said the priest. "What kind of children would be wandering about on such a night? Terrible parents, those children must have. The poor dears! Let us now say a prayer for them, that they pass safely through this storm."

The priest bowed his head and began to pray, a long ambling *please Lord we beseech thee* type of thing you could bet would last an hour at least.

"Come on now, none of that," said Mr. Hugo. "There'll be no praying now. We're trying to ask you a question."

"Then I shall pray in my heart, silently, so as not to distract you," said the priest. "Your questions, sirs?"

"What about your old pal Davey Boy Pennington? You seen him?" said Cecily Bob.

Wait, did the priest know Pop? How? I had never known Pop to be much of a churchgoer, though Mom loved church, even if it turned out she was a witch. Seemed like every time I learned something new about my folks the more questions I had. I guess that was the way of the world. Every time you get an answer to something you're wondering about, it just leads to more and more wondering. Maybe nothing ever truly gets answered. Maybe that's all life is, just wondering and wandering and hoping, maybe getting a thing or two right now and then.

"Davey Boy? My friend?" The priest bowed. "You do me honor sir. But nay, no Davey Boys here. Not a sighting, not a hide nor hair. Only stray cats here and there. Felines and owls. Snakes. Seen several snakes. They slither past the pulpit, yes. They be slithering past your ankles right now."

Mr. Hugo glanced down in a panic at the water rising around his knees. I heard Tally cover her mouth and snicker.

Cecily Bob drew out a knife, that same long one he pulled on my daddy. Cecily Bob poked at the priest with it. The priest giggled a little, like the knife tickled.

"I remember when you weren't stark raving mad," said Cecily Bob. "Do you remember that, priest? Do you remember a church full of the pious and holy?" He laughed, the sound slapping across the wet water room.

"I recall, yes sir," said the priest. "I do recall smiling faces gazing up at me from the pews."

"You gave quite a homily, I do declare," said Cecily Bob. "I myself attended several services. Was raised in the church you know, don't have much use for God, because God don't hex people. People hex people, they steal and murder and kill. God just sits up there and fumes about it, if ever he gives thought to us at all. Maybe he whips up a hurricane and sends it our way a few years down the line. Don't got nothing to do with me."

"I think you will find," said the priest, "that God is quite active in the world. Yes, I daresay he is the very thing holding the blood in your veins right now."

"He didn't keep us from torching your church though, did he?" said Mr. Hugo. "God didn't protect you from that."

"Perhaps," said the priest, his voice trembling just a little, "God did save his church." He knocked a hard rap on the pew with his fist. "The building of course is just a building, bricks and stone and wood. God's church is people, it is, and he is active in the hands and fingers that heal, in the mind and eyes and heart of those seeking justice." The priest held his arms out wide over the flooded church floor. "If ye squint even, perhaps you'll yet see God hovering over this very swamp right now."

The priest cocked a wide eye to the right and to the left, as if he might catch God unawares, tiptoeing across the water.

"You're a creepy old loon, you know that?" said Mr. Hugo. "We already ransacked Baudelaire Quatro's Place. Maybe we ought to burn your church a second time while we're at it."

"On a night like this," said the priest, sticking his bald head under a stream of water leaking down from a hole in the ceiling, "you might find it difficult. I doubt the wood would catch!"

"Cheeky too, he is," said Cecily Bob. "Might need to be taught a lesson there, eh Mr. Hugo?" He stroked the priest's neck with the knife. Then he yanked the bottom of the priest's beard and sawed it off in one swipe.

The priest fell over backward, cackling in the water.

"I'd wanted a shave!" he hollered, holding chunks of wet beard in his hands. "I've been meaning to see a barber! A barber in the swamp! You should go into business, the two of you!" He splashed in the water, laughing.

"Let's go, Mr. Hugo," said Cecily Bob. "The man's got too many bats in his belfry."

"Aye," said Mr. Hugo. "We'll get no truth out of him."

When they were good and gone, the priest looked up to where Tally and I hid in the rafters.

"You see that?" he said. "I foxed them, I did. I foxed them good."

Me and Tally made our way down to the pews, the water up to our waists now. The owls didn't hardly fluster. They just watched on, not even curious, like they already knew what was going to happen ages ago.

"Thanks for saving us," said Tally.

"That's my job, little one," said the priest. "Or it's supposed to be, anyhow. Can't say I've done too much saving the last few years. Glad to have the opportunity this evening."

"So you knew my daddy?" I said. "Davey Boy Pennington?"

"Of course I knew him!" he said. "I knew all of them, Sinclair and Marina and the rest. Being priest here used to mean something, I tell you. I had respect, I did, and those who came to me knew I would tell them the truth, and they were safe to receive it as they liked. I was also a magnificent cook, if I do say so myself. That brought folks around, when the sermons didn't." He leaned down to me. "I even blessed you, child, on the day you were born, if you can believe that."

Honestly, I wasn't sure if I could. I didn't remember much time in chapel, not when I was a kid, except getting bored and falling asleep in the pews. It made me happy, it did, to know that someone had blessed me along the way.

"Did you know Boss Authority too?" said Tally.

"Little Bobby Felix you mean?" The priest frowned. "Yes, I knew him. Quiet boy, he was. Sinclair was cruel to him, vicious even. They all were, except for your mother, Samantha Annie. Wild, she could be, but never cruel. Tell me, how does she fare these days?"

"Pretty good," I said. "She runs a bakery up in Collardsville."

"I do not know the place," said the priest. "Is it far beyond the swamp? I don't believe I've seen dry plains in nearly three decades now."

"Yep," I said. "Also I just found out she was a witch. Did you know she was a witch?"

"Samantha Annie? Of course I knew she was a witch," he said. "Only question is how in the world you didn't. I wager you ain't the sharpest fang in the mouth, are you?" He turned to Tally. "And now tell me, little one, is the secret you bear of your own doing, a hex, or is it inborn, in your blood?"

Tally flinched back, like she was trying to hide herself in the shadows.

"Oh don't be scared now," said the priest. "I am friend of spiders and humans alike. Any little critter, really, even the ones who mean me harm."

"I was born like this," said Tally. "Me and my granddad, though it skipped my parents."

"Extraordinary, what gifts are passed down in the blood," said the priest. "Fearful to some, yes, but they can also be a marvel. I see God's hand in all of this, child, do you not?"

"Easy for you to say when it ain't you that looks like a freak," said Tally.

"Freak? Freak?" said the priest. He whirled his arms around, pointing at the ruined church, the moldy walls, the cracked altar, the statues of saints slathered in bird droppings. "My child, there does not exist a beating heart that one could rightly call normal. We are all miraculous, each and every one of us. Miraculous and terrible, down to our darkest hearts. Seek the light, and the light shall burn out all the darkness. Seek the darkness, and yet, it cannot swallow all of the light. No, not even in the worst of us."

"I still don't like being spider-folk," said Tally.

"That, my dear, is your prerogative," said the priest. "But enough talk, enough idleness. Seems like we ought to get you two to Marina's Place. Though I don't think she'll cotton much to that Parsnit deck you're carrying."

"How'd you know I had Parsnit cards?" I said.

The priest held his hands together at his chest, like he was praying, and gave me a little bow.

"The cards? I can smell them from here," he said. "And Marina will sniff them out too." He twirled the stub of his beard with his fingers. "No, Marina won't like that one bit."

"Whoever heard of a witch who don't like Parsnit?" said Tally.

"Oh it's not that she doesn't like it, in some pure abstracted form," said the priest. "It's that she doesn't like what it has become." He bent down toward us and leaned in close, his eyes darting back and forth between Tally and me. "Want to know the secret about Parsnit cards?"

I nodded at him.

"They're just cards," he said. "Nothing more, nothing less."

"But they're magic," I said.

"Ah yes, magic and miracles, miracles and magic," he said. "It's all anybody ever wants, magic and miracles, miracles and magic." A blue-back damselfly flew up and landed on his outstretched finger. "As if all this ain't enough?" He blew on the damselfly and it flew away and into the night. Lightning bugs blinked all around him, haloing his head in the darkness.

Who was this man, this priest who knew Pop, who knew my mom? Who kept watch over his sunken ruined church, same as he had when it was pretty and filled with people instead of just owls and riffraff? The swamp was full of more wonders than I could fathom, and that was the truth of it.

"Come now," said the priest. "Let's find Miss Marina's. It is a safe place." He looked around sadly at his church. "Perhaps it is the last safe place, if Mr. Quatro's has fallen. Come children. We must hurry."

"What about my skiff?" I said.

"They will know it. No, no, we must take mine."

The priest led us through a burnt-out hole in the back of the church where a doorway probably once stood. A flat boat floated in a pool of water. It was patched and wretched-looking. Spiders flung their webs all over the bottom, and little water droplets hung everywhere in glimmers. It was the sorriest excuse for a boat I'd ever seen in my life.

"Does it float?" said Tally. "I mean, when it has people in it?"

"It's floated longer than you've been on this earth, child. And it'll float ages more." The priest held a couple of mildewed sacks out toward us. "Crouch down and hide, crawl into these. We must pretend you are potatoes, yes? We must pretend you are ears and ears of corn. For the orphans, yes, a donation from the church. Why not? Why not?"

"But they'll find us," I said. "All they got to do is yank this sack off us and we're done for."

"They won't dare," said the priest, "because I shall be preaching. And they hate my preaching, yes they do. It afears them, I do believe. Or perhaps it just annoys. Whichever case, it'll do nicely."

We brushed the spiderwebs away and crawled into the boat and stuffed ourselves into the sacks. The priest poled us out into the swamp water. I had a nice eye-sized hole in my sack, just big enough to see through. The rain had stopped, and the night was all foggy and cloudy, barely a wink of moon up there, stars peeking out where you could see them. Deep in the distance burned what looked like bonfires.

"They do that when a prisoner's on the loose," said the priest. "When they're after someone important."

"They're hunting us," said Tally.

"Yeah," I said, "but mostly I bet they're looking for Pop."

"It's a takeover, it is," said the priest. "Bobby Felix is finally having his revenge on the swamp."

The priest pushed us away from the church, handling the long wooden pole like it wasn't more than a twig. I realized he was strong too, this skin-and-bone priest, that he was something mighty hidden in rags. We left the narrow path and drifted into open water as far as the eye could see. Big bonfires burning on the high ground, on any dry knee of sand and dirt that rose out of the water. From holes in the sack we saw boats with torches passing, Boss Authority's men scanning the waters. The priest poled us right up next to a canoe with two mean-looking fellas in it. One of them had an eye patch and a long cruel scar across his throat. He spat in the water as our boat came near to him.

The priest stood up tall in the boat. He leapt from foot to foot, rocking us wildly, and for a minute I was scared we would tip.

"Repent!" cackled the priest, his voice gone high and wily. "Repent and be saved! Cast off the old man, the flesh, the sickness of spirit! Wash yourself in the blood, I say! Cover yourself in the mercy of the divine father! He is not angry with them who seek mercy, no, his loving kindness endureth forever. But woe to you, rich! Woe to you, greedy and unmerciful! Woe to you, liars and thieves! Woe to you who would defraud the widow and the orphan, who would lie to those in need!"

"Be quiet, you old psycho," said the man with the eye

patch. "We're trying to work here."

"But where will the mercy be for you, sir, when judgment comes?" said the priest.

"Only judgment comes from Boss Authority," said the man, "and if you don't hush your geezer old yapper, then I'll have to shut you up myself."

"Mercy!" cried the priest. He fell to the floor of the boat. "Mercy please, on an old man!" He covered his face and bowed his head, all meek and terrified. He tossed me and Tally a wink.

"Just get out of here already," said the man. "We're out hunting, and you don't want to get in the way when we find what we're looking for."

"Be blessed!" hollered the priest. "Blessed be ye in the name of the Lord!"

And he poled us onward.

"I can't tell if this guy's crazy," whispered Tally, "or if he's some kind of genius."

"What's the difference, so long as we get safe to Marina's?" I said.

The night had gone low-down and spooky after the storm. A slit of moon burned above us, and only the brightest stars, clouds skimming over them like ghosts. Here and there the bonfires cast their glow, and Boss Authority's men swept through the swamp, silent and watchful, their torches a burning warning to us in our hiding. But no one bothered checking the priest's boat, no one bothered with the skinny bald man ranting and hollering about salvation. I realized the priest was his own kind of hustler, the same as me and Tally, same as the magician, same as Pop. Maybe he was hustling for a better cause—the salvation of the world ain't exactly something to shake your head at—but he was putting on a show all the same.

We watched a man get yanked from an old stilt house. He was a tall fella with red hair, and two of Boss Authority's men flung him into their boat, facedown while his wife and child hollered on, crying.

"What did he do?" I said.

"Looks like Boss Authority's rounding up anyone he thinks might be an enemy," said the priest. "This is the fifth anniversary of your daddy's defeat, is it not? This is his hour, unless your pop steps up and does something."

The man in the boat tried to stand, and Boss Authority's men whomped him in the head with a club. He went slack, groaning from the floor of the boat.

The priest started singing then, a sweet high lovely song like it came out of a mountain, a cold song like the wind blew it straight down from a snow-covered peak, another song of hope and mourning. It wasn't a swamp song at all, no sir, it wasn't born in these parts, and you knew it had traveled a long way to get here. Boss Authority's men paused from beating the fella in the boat and they perked up to listen, watching us pass in the priest-poled skiff, his song soft as fog among the waters. It was as if he stilled the moment, as if all the world had frozen and it was only us in this boat sliding like a lily pad across the water. I wondered if the priest didn't have some kind of magic to him as well, or if that was just music, what music could do to any heart and mind, so long as the person had ears to hear it.

Where was Pop though? Why wasn't he doing something to stop all this? Folks were hurting, folks were bound up and arrested, and anyone who wasn't was scared out of their minds. I knew Pop was in the swamp somewhere, I knew he'd escaped from Cecily Bob and Mr. Hugo. Then why wasn't he out here, fighting Boss Authority's men? Why hadn't he challenged Boss Authority to a rematch? Boy, would I love to see that, Pop finally whoop Boss Authority in a Parsnit duel for the ages. I wished he would show already. I wished Tally and me didn't have to slink through the waters hidden on a crazy man's boat just to get us to safety. And judging from what the priest said about Marina's feelings on Parsnit, maybe her place wouldn't be safe after all, at least not for me, son of Davey Boy Pennington.

Onward the priest poled us, deeper and deeper into the swamp. My leg got a cramp in it, and somehow a mosquito got into the sack. He was right going to town on me, probably drank near a gallon of my blood, but I didn't dare slap him away. All around us the swamp was alive and humming, a wild, breathing place. I felt like we had been swallowed by some big ol' beast and we were floating around in its stomach, warm and dark, a whole world down here in the great belly of everything.

"Come now, children," whispered the priest. "We're here."

I peeked up out of my burlap sack and saw it, Marina's Place. It was a big stilt lodge-looking thing, much bigger than I thought. It stretched for rooms and rooms, maybe two hundred feet long and lord knows how far back it went. Some sections of it looked newer than others, like Marina had been busy building more space for herself. I wondered what she would be like, this mighty witch. I wondered if she wouldn't catch a glance at Pop's Parsnit deck and chuck me right back out on my face in the muck.

"Out, out, children!" said the priest. "And hurry. Folks'll be along here soon enough, and that's a fact. Yes, they'll even come to Marina's, for murder or for sanctuary, you can bet on it. Inside, quickly."

"Aren't you coming with us?" said Tally. I could tell she was a little bit scared of Marina too.

"No, no," he said. "A priest doesn't seek refuge, he offers it. So I'm off into the waters, to help where I can. Blessings, children, and God be with you."

We climbed up to Marina's porch, standing before her thick shut massive front doors, scared to push them open, while the priest poled off into the fog and the dark.

I was scared, you bet I was. Cecily Bob and Mr. Hugo were armed and after us, my pop was missing in the swamp, and there didn't seem to be too much hope left for us. I looked up at the sky and said my own kind of prayer. The clouds were long gone now, all the stars like little old ladies peeking from dark windows. Oh yes, tonight had some magic to it, it had a shimmer of luck glistening in the mucky water. I just hoped that good luck was enough to counter my own.

I took me a deep breath and shoved the door open, and together me and Tally stepped inside.

15

THE DOORS OPENED TO A high-roofed room, like some kind of banquet hall, or a restaurant I guess. The room was maybe a hundred feet across, with tables scattered around, folks milling about here and there. Two ancient men sat at one of the tables, a black man and a white fella, laughing at their own jokes. One of them carried a rusty old war sword on his belt. A piano player banged away on an upright in the corner. Lines of strung lizards and baby gators hung behind an empty bar, and a huge fierce fish was mounted on the wall in what appeared to be a striking pose, fangs jutting from its jaw like broken shards of bone. I recognized some of the people from Baudelaire Quatro's. A couple were wounded and bandaged, but there they stood, alive and together.

There were doors in the back and to the left and right, leading to different rooms where people came and went freely. This seemed like a safe spot, Marina's Place. You could hide here, protected, like the priest said, and it felt as if even Boss Authority couldn't touch you. It was sparse and lantern-lit, but cheerful a little bit, like the two old men there had been sitting quite happy in these exact same spots the last five years and they'd still be here five years later. On a red cushion in the far end of the room lay a bearded man in overalls, curled up and drooling like a dog, sleeping soft on a pillow. When we burst in he poked his head up and blinked at me a few times, then settled back down asleep.

"You got to help us," I said. "Folks are after us."

"Folks, say you?" said one of the old guys. I nodded. "Lawrence, this young fella says he has folks after him."

"Aye," said Lawrence. "I have ears as well, lest ye forget."

"Hard to forget with that racket out back, eh?" He pointed to the piano player.

"He should learn some new songs, say I, instead of bashing about with the same old same old. I tire of 'Dirty Blue Boots,' do you not, Johnson?"

"Aye, sir. I am weary to the bone."

"Please," said Tally. "You got to help us. These folks after us mean business. They're dangerous, they got knives, they got—"

"Knives, you say?" said Lawrence. "Well let them come.

We fear not knives, do we Johnson?"

"Nay," said Johnson. "I've been stabbed two and twenty times, and yet I walk, do I not Lawrence?"

"I would say you hobble, dear sir, and with the aid of a cane."

"Too true. Hear hear!" said Johnson, and slapped the table. The two old men raised their mugs and drank.

This was durn useless. Cecily Bob and Mr. Hugo were probably going to be here any minute and I would be tied up and slung back in a boat, on my way once again to Boss Authority. That I simply could not abide.

"Perhaps the children would like some food?" said Johnson. "Shall we offer them some?"

"Aye, Johnson," said Lawrence. "Splendid idea. Victuals, children?"

"*We are in danger,*" said Tally, slowly, deliberately. "What about that don't you understand? This is no time for food."

"No time for food! Danger is the perfect time for dining," he said. "Keeps the appetite low and the heart rate high, I say!"

"He speaks facts, Johnson does," said Lawrence. "You would do well to listen to him. As it stands, Johnson and I have just ordered dinner, and we would be delighted if you could join us."

A short man in a stained apron and a chef's hat came walking out of the back, carrying a giant steel platter with a barbecued hog on it. The hog had an apple in its mouth and it looked durn proud to be there, I must say. The man dropped the hog on the old men's table with a thunk.

"Capital hog!" said Lawrence, tying a napkin around his neck.

"He looks positively delighted," said Johnson, clapping his hands. "The finest hog yet, Stanley my good sir."

"Caught him myself," said Stanley. "He was out back, grunting through the waters. Charged at me, he did, with them tusks of his. Near took my arm off!"

"I should salute you, sir," said Lawrence, "with twelve guns or more."

"A ticker tape parade," said Johnson. "Wouldn't that be nice? Like we had after the war."

"Aye, those were the days," said Lawrence. "A hero's welcome in every shop, a mug uplifted in every tavern. Drink, drink, Johnson. To our youth!"

"To our youth!"

They both drank deep.

A black woman walked out from the back, about six-and-a-half feet tall in her boots. She had a half-shaved head, and she wore trousers and a no-sleeved shirt. Her arms were all muscled and covered with tattoos—symbols and words in languages I didn't know and pictures of all kinds of stuff, trees and flowers and daggers and pages from old books—like there was some great history of everything scribbled on her skin.

"Were y'all just gonna sit there yapping or were you going to introduce me to our guests?" she said.

"Aye, sorry Miss Marina," said Johnson. "We were distracted by this magnificent oinker here." He peered at me, adjusting his glasses. "I didn't catch your name, lad."

"I'm Buddy," I said. "And this here's Tally. There's folks after us. We're in serious danger."

"Hear that, Miss Marina?" said Lawrence. "These little fellows are wanted."

"Positively felons!" said Johnson.

"Not only wanted, these two," said Marina. "Something smells a bit off about them."

"Well I ain't bathed in a few days," I said. "Except in swamp water."

"I ain't talking about your body odor," said Marina. "What say you, Harlen?"

The dog-seeming man on the cushion lifted his head and howled, long and mournful.

"That's what I thought." Marina walked toward me, her boots clomping on the hardwood floor. "There's a tinge around you, like crushed flowers, like the month after a funeral. A sad smell. Melancholy. Boy, I daresay there is magic afoot here. You're hexed, you are. And there's something particular about her." Marina pointed to Tally. "But no, that's not what I'm smelling. That's not it at all."

She grabbed my knapsack.

"There are cards in here," she said. "Parsnit cards." The lanterns in the room dimmed, the candles flickered, and a cool wind seemed to sweep across the floor. "You've brought Parsnit cards into Marina's Place?"

The tables began to shake, spilling drink all over the two old men. They hollered, grabbing onto the pork so as it wouldn't slop off on the ground.

"I'm sorry," I said. "We didn't know. We didn't mean anything by it."

"There will be no apologies," said Marina, her voice low and booming, her eyes gone black and empty, her hair standing on end as if lightning struck. "Those infernal cards are not allowed here, and that is well known. Who would dare to bring a Parsnit deck in my house?"

Fire flashed inside the room and smoke billowed up from beneath the floorboards, like it was rising from the swamp, like Hell itself had gathered about us and was seeping in through the floor.

"It's okay, Marina," said a man's voice. "Those cards are mine."

A silhouette leaned against the piano in the back of the room, lingering in the shadows a little bit. He seemed tired, grizzled, a few days' beard growth on his cheeks, a little slouch to him. But when he walked toward me he had that same strut I recognized, the one I tried to imitate my whole life, and when he smiled that big gold-toothed smile at me, there wasn't any doubt who I was looking at.

"Pop!" I said, and ran toward him.

He picked me up and spun me and held me close to him, same as he had when I was just a kid, same as he had my whole life. I loved my pop so much in that moment I didn't hardly have words for it.

"How the heck did you get down here, Buddy?" he said. "I thought you were a goner. I thought when Mr. Hugo blew that skiff up, I'd lost you forever."

"You kidding? Not me, Pop," I said. "I found my own boat. I came after you. Me and Tally here."

He walked over to Tally.

"You help save my boy's life?" he said.

"Yep," I said. "She saved my life twice already."

"Well then, little lady," said Pop, bowing low to her, "I am forever in your debt."

"Nah," said Tally, all awkward-like. "We saved each other."

"That sounds about like what real friends do," said Pop. "I should know. I got at least one of them left." He glanced over at Marina, who glared fierce back at him. "This place is safe. Marina's got magic guarding it, keeping ill-intentioned folks out, and that magic's even stronger than the witch's bond holding her in here. But that being said, I think it's best if you and me hit the trails, Buddy."

"Whatcha mean?" I said.

"I don't know if you noticed," he said, "but old Bobby Felix is on the move, he is. This whole swamp is his for the taking, and I for one am not going to stand here and be took. The magic will hold, but not for long, and not for the likes of me, being in dutch to Bobby Felix like I am."

"But that's why you're going to make a stand, right?" I said. "You're going to challenge him to another game of Parsnit, a rematch. I brought your cards and everything."

"Well, Buddy, not exactly," said Pop. "There's some extenuating circumstances that complicate this grand scheme of yours."

"You ought to tell him," said Marina. "You ought to tell your own boy the whole story."

"I know the story," I said. "Sinclair told me."

"Y'all met old Sinclair, eh?" said Pop.

"Yeah," said Tally. "The Creepy. He almost ate us. He almost ripped us to pieces."

"Well that's what I'm talking about," said Pop. "It's all my fault, you know that? And that's why we got to get you out of here."

"No way," I said. "Boss Authority just got lucky. He beat you once, no big deal. You can beat him this time, I'm sure of it. I mean, what have you been up to the last five years except training, getting every bit as good at Parsnit as a person can be? That's why you didn't come back home, right? That's why Mom had gone and left you, took me with her. She was sick of being second fiddle to a card game. She just must not have understood how important it was to keep fighting for your home, even when bad folks have taken it over. You didn't give up hope, but she did. That's why I'll never forgive her. That's why . . ."

"Buddy, you shut your mouth about your mom right now," he said. "She didn't give up on this place. She didn't give up on me. I let her down. I let both of you down."

"I don't understand, Pop," I said.

"That last Parsnit duel with Bobby Felix," he said, "the one I lost good and square, the one that doomed us all. I was pretty overconfident, you understand?"

"Arrogant is the word I would use," said Marina.

"Fine, fine," said Pop. "I was arrogant. I was as arrogant as the day is long. I figured there wasn't any way on earth I could be beat, especially not by puny little Bobby Felix. So when he set the terms of our duel, I accepted them outright. What he made me bet . . . what I agreed to bet . . . well. Buddy, I don't know how to say it. I was just so sure I would win. I didn't even think. I didn't even consider the cost."

"What did you bet?" I said.

"I bet the lives of my friends," he said. "I bet Marina's

exile to this house, never to set foot in the swamp again. I bet Sinclair to become the Creepy, a folktale passed down to scare kids to death."

"What about you?" I said. "What did you bet about you and Mom?"

"I left your mom out of this, I did," said Pop. "Bobby Felix wouldn't have nothing to do with harming your mom, and that's a fact. Your mom crying and pleading with Bobby Felix is the only way I left with the blood still in my veins."

"You mean you bet your blood, Pop?" I said. "Your own lucky blood?"

"More or less," said Pop.

"Tell him," said Marina. "The boy has a right to know. Tell him the exact wording of your witch's bond."

"According to what I pledged," said Pop, "I bet every drop of my blood on this earth. Every single drop."

I heard Tally gasp over in the corner. The two old men sat staring close at me, and the pianist had stopped his banging. They were all keyed in to this conversation, all of them hanging on every word. I heard a bat chitter on the ceiling of Marina's Place, and all else was still, all else was silent, all else understood what I still didn't.

"But Pop," I said, "that means the next time he sees you, you're done for. I get it. And that's why you got to leave."

"It ain't me I'm worried about," he said. "It's you. See, I bet all my blood on this earth, every last drop. You're half me, aren't you? Half that blood in your veins is mine, at least in magic terms. Boss Authority has every right to drain you dry, Buddy. That's why your mom fled the Riverlands, to keep you as far away from Bobby Felix's power as possible. That's why I left my Parsnit deck with you that night, instead of lugging it along. I was hoping that maybe I would have a chance of survival if I hid out in Marina's. Heck, Buddy, that's why I had you hexed by the most powerful witch in these lands, Marina here, to curse your blood, so it wouldn't be any use to Bobby Felix."

"You had me hexed, Pop?" I said.

I couldn't believe it. There wasn't any way. My pop would never do that to me. He would never.

"I did, Buddy," said Pop. "I had your blood hexed so maybe Boss Authority would let you alone. Hexed blood is a mighty dangerous thing."

I was mad now, I was durn furious.

"Let me get this straight," I said. "You're telling me the reason my life's been so terrible these past five years is you, my own daddy? You're the reason I couldn't make a friend, why I couldn't so much as kick a ball without twisting an ankle? Why I nearly burned Mom's bakery down on accident, almost killing the both of us? It's your fault my whole life has been one durn miserable disaster after another?"

"Buddy," said Tally. "It's okay. If he made the hex, he can break it. Right?" She turned to Marina. "That's how a hex works. It's no problem for the person who made it to break it."

"I got it right here," said Pop. He pulled a piece of dried vine looped in a knot that hung from a string around his neck. "This here's the hex. All I got to do is snap this vine in half and you're free, Buddy boy, with half the luckiest blood on earth and half good-witch magic to you. Heck, your blood is more valuable to Bobby Felix—more powerful that is—even than mine. So I ain't gonna snap this vine. No sir. That hex is what's kept you alive this long. I'm sorry it has been a trial on you, I really am. But there was no other choice, Buddy. There was no other way of keeping you safe."

I couldn't believe it. This whole time, years and years, I thought Mom had wrecked my life. I thought Mom had run out on Pop, that she'd been jealous and mean. But it had been Pop's fault all along. Everything bad was his fault. He had hexed me, he'd made our home unsafe, he'd . . . he'd bet my own blood against Boss Authority. Pop had risked my life, not just his, and he hadn't even asked me, it hadn't even occurred to him that he'd lose. How could my own daddy be so reckless, how could he risk my life like that, and the lives of all his friends, without hardly a thought, without a single worry in his mind?

"Did Mom know?" I asked.

"Of course your mom knew," he said. "And she was durn furious at me for it. Said her magic was more than enough to protect you, if I'd just trust her. But I had to take care of it myself, you understand? I had to make absolutely sure you were spoiled for Boss Authority. I begged her not to tell you, and I guess she kept her word." He shook his head. "That's just like Samantha Annie. She was probably up all hours of the night trying to break that hex on you, I wouldn't doubt it. I bet she never let up trying, even if it was useless."

That's what Mom was going to tell me after I burned the bakery down, wasn't it? That was the talk we were going to have the next day, the one where I wouldn't like what I was going to hear. Mom wasn't mad at me at all. She was mad at Pop.

"You can hate me all you want, Buddy," said Pop. "We got years and years for that kind of thing. And it's okay, I deserve it. But for now, we got to go, and quick." He grabbed my hand and yanked me toward the back of Marina's. "There's a side door, a whole escape route I figured. If we hustle we can clear the swamp in a few days, take to the road after that. Any luck, we can get free. Any luck we'll be clear before Boss Authority knows otherwise."

"What about Tally?" I said.

"She'll be fine," said Pop. "Marina will take good care of her, won't you, Marina?"

"Now just wait one second," said Marina.

"No time, no time!" said Pop.

"But what about the swamp?" I said. "What about all the

folks getting taken by Boss Authority? What about everyone who's gonna suffer after he gets all his power?"

"Right now, Buddy," said Pop, "my only concern is you. Call it selfish, call it good parenting, call it whatever you want. I got one duty as a parent, and that's to get you to safety."

I yanked my hand from his and stood tall as I could to face my daddy, to stare him right in his eyes.

"Well you already blew that," I said. "You blew that five years ago. I don't think you got any right to tell me what to do anymore. I don't think you got any right to say a single word to me one way or the other."

Pop looked like I'd just sucker punched him one in the gut. He looked grizzled and tired, and for just one second that sparkle left his gold tooth and his smile failed, it withered right there on his face. I saw him clearly then, maybe for the first time. How skinny he'd gotten, how haggard and hungry. How his hair was thinning in the front, all the scars on his arms, a fresh gleaming one on his cheek. Pop was old, he was, and he looked beaten. He wasn't one bit the legend I'd made him in my mind. No sir, my daddy was a person, same as any other. A sorry person, at that. I'd never seen a sadder sight in all my life.

The dog-looking fella leapt onto his feet and gave a growl.

"What are you smelling, Harlen?" said Marina. "What

do you sniff out there on the wind?"

"Must be the pursuers!" said Lawrence. "Up, up Johnson! We may yet be of use!"

The two old fellas hobbled to their feet and the piano player got to hammering away and my daddy stood stock-still, a look of terror on his face like I'd never seen before once in my whole life. Tally grabbed my hand and I held hers tight, grateful for her yet again, grateful to feel the little hairs sprouting up on her palm as the spider in her began to show itself.

The lights flickered again, and this time it wasn't of Marina's doing, no sir. This time it was something else.

The doors flung open, and there he stood, Bobby Felix, Boss Authority himself. Cecily Bob and Mr. Hugo to his left, Drusilla Fey on his right. They had come finally to Marina's Place, just waltzed right in through that magic like it was nothing. They had finally come for my pop.

They had come for me.

16

BOSS AUTHORITY STOOD SMALL AND monstrous in the doorway, his boots clanking on the floor, that great clockwork fist grinding and whirring. He was scarred and foul and weird-eyed, and just his presence in the room made all my hairs stand on end, all the magic he carried with him.

The room cleared. I mean, folks scattered, whether to the infinite backrooms of Marina's Place or out into the swamp itself, I didn't have a clue. Fact is, they fled, and they fled fast, and wasn't hardly anybody left in that room except us.

"Marina, my dear. It's been too long," said Boss Authority.

"It's only been five years, Bobby Felix," said Marina. "Barely a blink of an eye."

"And my old pal Davey Boy," he said, clapping his hands

together. The metal one donged like a church bell.

"Bobby," said Pop, nodding his head, grinning as best as he could.

"The rest of these fellas I ain't acquainted with," said Boss Authority. He clomped through the room toward me and Tally.

"These are just two kids I picked up," said Marina. "Strays that done lost their way."

"Strays, huh? Well children, you sure picked the wrong place and the wrong time to be there."

"That's my luck," I said. "It's my durn hexed luck," and I shot Pop a look ugly enough to shatter glass.

Harlen the dog-man crept on all fours toward Boss Authority and let out a low growl.

"You best call that fella off," said Boss Authority, "whatever ails him."

Marina whistled and Harlen came running back to her. She scratched him behind his ears. Harlen rolled over on his back and she rubbed the belly of his ragged overalls.

"Dog-brained," said Lawrence. "That's what ails him, Mr. Boss."

"Dogness is an improvement," said Johnson. "I knew him back in the war!"

"You mean to tell me this man here wasn't always canine-inclined?" said Boss Authority.

"I'm saying this is my place, Bobby Felix," said Marina,

"and in my place you treat me with respect."

"You always did have a penchant for dogs," said Drusilla Fey.

"And you never could keep your traitor mouth shut," said Marina. "I don't know how you got in here at all. My magic should have kept out the both of you, until the sun burned out and all the stars crashed in on themselves."

"Could be you were that powerful, say five years ago," said Boss Authority. "But things change, Marina. Times change. I change." He brought his clockwork hand up and wiggled the fingers, his long ponytail swishing back and forth like a snake.

"I don't think I like your attitude," said Marina. "I don't think I like the way you disrespect my house."

Marina's tattoos began to glow. It was like she had embers under her skin, the way the lines lit up and flared, like they'd burn you if you reached out and touched them.

"Drusilla, if you don't mind," said Boss Authority.

She licked her lips, her tongue forked like a snake's. "My pleasure, darlin'."

Drusilla Fey floated up off the ground, her bare feet lifted, her toenails scratching the floor. Her fingernails grew, they stretched out like bone claws. She clacked them together and it sounded like a snake's rattle. For one moment she hovered, strange and fluttery, in the air. We all held our breath, everyone in the room, as the two witches squared off, waiting.

The next bit all happened at once.

Drusilla Fey let out a shriek and flew toward Marina.

Mr. Hugo and Cecily Bob drew knives and came for Pop. The coward tried to run, he did. I was never more ashamed in my life.

Harlen snapped at Boss Authority and Boss backhanded him down, that clockwork hand dinging through the room.

Me and Tally backed up to where the pianist crouched hidden behind his piano. Tally was full spider and ready to fight, and so was I as much as that was worth, but neither of us knew quite what to do.

"We could probably get Pop free from Mr. Hugo and Cecily Bob, but I don't want to risk those knives," I said.

Drusilla Fey had Marina on the ground, three of her fingernails snapped off and stuck through Marina's clothes like daggers, fixing her to the floor.

"It's the tattoos, ain't it, Drusilla?" said Boss Authority. "It's the tattoos that's the source of her power." Boss Authority's face grimaced like he'd been sucking on a lemon all day. "I want her power. I want those tattoos."

He ripped the sleeve off his jacket, his pale, scarred arm all muscles and veins, not a thing natural about it.

Lawrence stepped creakily toward Boss Authority, his war blade drawn and ready. "You have disturbed the peace of my old age, fiend!" he said. "Unhand Miss Marina!"

"Give him what's coming, Lawrence!" said Johnson.

Boss Authority grabbed the blade in his fist and snapped it in half. Then he pushed the old man backward onto the floor.

"Lawrence!" hollered Johnson. He hobbled over and knelt by his friend.

"I can't just sit here and watch," said Tally. She skittered herself up the wall of Marina's Place. In a second Tally was up on the ceiling, hissing at them, her fangs out and ready. She was way braver than I was, and that was a fact.

Cecily Bob and Mr. Hugo pinned Pop down, had him hogtied, with a bucket ready, like they were going to string him up and drain him right then and there, gather every last drop of his lucky blood. Tally leapt off the ceiling and landed right on Mr. Hugo's back, sinking her fangs deep in his neck. Cecily Bob whipped out a knife and came after Tally, trying to stab her off Mr. Hugo's back. That just about did it for me. I picked up a wooden stool and came charging at him, screaming loud as I could. I chucked it at Cecily Bob and it smashed right into his back.

The stool didn't do hardly a thing except make him drop his knife. Cecily Bob turned around and kicked me so hard in the chest I went flying, the wind knocked clean out of me. I lay on the floor, helpless as could be.

I watched as Drusilla Fey's left-hand fingernails went clicking all over Marina's arm, and her right fingernails went to work on Boss Authority's arm. The markings began to disappear on Marina's arm, to fade and blur and vanish, and reappear just the same on Boss Authority's arm. He was stealing her magic, he was. Drusilla Fey was leeching it out of Marina and straight onto his skin. Soon the tattoos were gone, Marina's arm blank of symbols and scratchings, not a lick of ink on them.

"My mom gave me those tattoos," said Marina, crouched in a huddle on the ground. "It was the last thing I had of her."

I saw Mr. Hugo fling Tally off his bleeding back, saw her scuttle to a corner. I saw my daddy strung up by Cecily Bob, all his lucky blood soon to be drained out. I saw Harlen limp toward Marina, the two of them huddled together in pain and anger on the floor. I saw Lawrence sprawled out on his back, Johnson helping him up to his chair. I saw the durn cowardly pianist inching toward the rear door, and me right there next to him. Everybody else had fled from Marina's Place.

We had lost, all of us. The last safe place in the Swamplands had fallen. Pop was captured. Tally was still spider-folk. And no one, not a single person in this room, was paying one lick of attention to me one way or the other.

I was about durn sick of that.

I looked around the room, at all the folks I knew and loved, at the ones who I figured were against Boss Authority and on my side. Every single one of them was a hustler.

That was just a fact. Every one of those folks had their own game running, in one way or another. They all had an angle, they were all smart and brave, I knew they all had their own plan running quick in the back of their minds. I just needed to give them a little room to operate, that was all. What did Pop say that first night I came to visit him, when he pulled that card trick on me? He said the problem was I was watching him the whole time, didn't he? That I would understand later. Well maybe I got it now. Maybe magic is what happens when everyone's looking somewhere else. That was a true hustler's trick it was, just like Tally did when she was fake-begging, what the priest did when he smuggled us across the waters. I just needed to give Boss and his folks something else to look at, distract them enough to give my people room to work.

I staggered up to my feet, the air back in my lungs, my body hurt but with nothing broken.

"Listen up!" I hollered.

Nobody paid me any notice, same as usual. That right about ticked me off. I cupped my hands and gave it all my lungs could give.

"I said shut up, everybody! Boss Authority, you faker! You, having to steal other folks' magic because you ain't got any of your own. That's right I'm talking to you. Listen up now, or you'll be sorry."

"You say I'll be sorry?" said Boss Authority. "I don't think I got much to fear from a little scamp like you."

"Shoot, you ain't much taller than me," I said, swaggering toward him like I figured Pop would, poking my chest out, faking brave as best as I could. "Figured if you didn't have a metal hand and that goofy snake ponytail, I could probably whoop you in a fair fight myself."

That got him, it did. Boss Authority took the bait. He walked *clank clomp* right over to me, stared me down eye to eye.

"Give me one reason not to slit you gut to gizzard, little man," he said.

"You play Parsnit, Boss?" I said.

"'Course I play Parsnit," he said. "Ain't a better Parsnit player on this whole earth than me, and that's a fact. Just ask that fella strung up over there."

He laughed, pointing at my daddy. I couldn't look at Pop, not if I wanted to keep myself from crying. So I didn't, I kept my eyes right on Boss Authority, I pulled all the grit and bluster I could into my voice and faked it with every bit of might and power I had.

"I ain't got to ask him," I said, "because he's my no-good rotten lying scoundrel daddy."

"That a fact?" asked Boss Authority. "You his runt, all grown up?"

"I am," I said. "And what's more, I'm ten times the Parsnit player he ever dreamed of being. Besides, I'm blood ain't I? Parsnit rules say I can take over his bet if I want. I can be his rematch."

"But what can you offer me?" said Boss Authority. "Look around you. I already got everything I want."

"True," I said. "But you won half my lucky blood off Pop already, the luckiest blood on this earth."

Boy was I laying it on thick.

"Well, if you wound up here, I don't think it's half so lucky as you think."

"It is," I said. "But the other half of my blood is magic, thanks to my mom the witch. That half you don't own, not yet. Besides, that piano player who just bolted out the back door? He heard me challenge you. What's he going to tell the swamp, that Boss Authority was too scared to accept a duel from Davey Boy's son and heir? That he was afeared of some 'little runt' as you said?"

"You got grit, boy," he said. "I'll give you that."

I felt a tingling on my neck, like cold water dripping down my spine. I heard a rasping little voice in my ear, a voice I recognized. Marina.

What are you up to? she whispered right into my mind.

I'm buying you time, I thought back, as hard as I could.

"House rules say a challenge must be accepted," said

Marina, out loud where everybody could hear.

"This ain't Baudelaire Quatro's spot, last time I checked," said Boss Authority. "You don't even allow Parsnit here."

"I do now," said Marina. "It's my Place, it's my rules, and I just changed them. So long as this house stands, I still have a say in what goes on. And I say you have to accept."

Marina needn't have bothered. From what they'd told me about Boss Authority, he was wild about magic, he couldn't get enough of it. I remembered the wore-out folks at Baudelaire Quatro's, the folks who couldn't get enough magic. I figured Boss Authority was crazier about magic than all of them put together. He couldn't resist a game with me, Davey Boy's son and heir. He couldn't resist the opportunity to humiliate my pop all over again.

"I don't like it, Boss," said Mr. Hugo. "It's got to be some kind of jackpot."

"Kindly, Hugo, shut your durn mouth," said Boss Authority. "If I want your opinion on the matter, I will ask for it. Drusilla, can you handle Marina here?"

"Handle her? I could eat her up and spit her out," said Drusilla Fey. "I could drink her bones dry."

"Then what have we got to fear?" said Boss Authority. He turned to me. "I'm game, boy, if you are."

Pop was struggling against his gag, kicking and groaning.

"Looks like your old daddy's got something he wants to

tell you," said Boss Authority. "Let him loose, Mr. Hugo."

Mr. Hugo sliced the rope they had my pop strung up by, but since his hands were bound he couldn't catch himself and smashed headfirst onto the floor. It busted his noggin open a little, and I could tell it hurt. I hated watching them hurt Pop, I hated it just about more than I could hate anything on this earth, even if I was outright angry with him at the moment. But I couldn't let any of that show now. I had to keep a cool head, see if I could get Pop to see things my way.

"You can't let him play," said Pop. "He's just a boy."

"But he's your boy," said Boss Authority. "That gives him every right to play. Law by blood, ain't that what they call it, Drusilla Fey?"

"I believe that's just what it is, Boss," she said, her eyes flashing black in the lamplight. "Blood is the law we call upon, yes indeed."

"Buddy," said Pop, "what in the sam hill do you think you're doing?"

"I'm about to play some Parsnit," I said.

"You're going to get yourself killed is what you're doing," he said, "and it'll be all my fault. It'll be every bit my fault."

"Nah," I said. "I learned from the best, didn't I? And I'm making my own decision now. I got my own luck, don't I? It'll come through for me in the right time, that I do reckon, so long as it's free to."

Pop's eyes got wide then and I think he understood I had something cooking, I think he understood that I was hustling and scheming with every bit of craft I had. I caught the slightest gleam of his gold tooth, and yeah, Pop knew what I was up to.

"Just go easy on him, Bobby Felix," said Pop. "He's just a boy."

"Oh you know me," said Boss Authority. "I'm nothing if not a man of mercy."

Mr. Hugo and Cecily Bob and Drusilla Fey got to laughing at that. I for one didn't see the humor in it.

"Fine," I said, trying to keep my voice from shaking. "I win, you let me and all my friends go. You abandon your magics and skedaddle."

"That's an awful lot for me to wager," said Boss Authority.

"What's the point of playing," I said, "if you can't win big?"

Boss Authority got a chuckle out of that. "I like the way you think, boy. You remind me a little of myself at your age, if you can imagine that."

"I would prefer not to," I said.

"Got a mouth on you too," said Boss, rubbing his chin with his metal finger. "Well, fine. If I win, I get your daddy's blood—which is already mine by right, mind you—and I get your blood, and what else? How about a bottle of poison from the fangs of that one over there? Actually, I want the fangs themselves. I want her face for my collection."

"I don't think that's mine to wager," I said.

"It's done," said Tally. "You can have it, Boss."

"And you can have Marina's Place," said Marina.

"Marina, honey, it appears your house is already mine," said Boss.

"No it ain't," said Marina. "This place doesn't obey anybody but me. The second I walk out of here the whole thing will shutter itself and sink right into the swamp, whether you want it to or not. Same as what happened to Baudelaire Quatro's. By the way, what did you do with his head?"

"I kept it," Boss said, "same as I'm going to keep yours. I'm gonna pickle it, Marina. I'm going to keep it right there on my mantel. It'll be one heck of a conversation piece."

"We'll see about that," said Marina, wiping a trickle of blood from her chin.

I wasn't sure how much I liked this now. I was feeling like maybe they were putting a bit too much faith in me. I was fine playing for myself and my blood, but I didn't feel too good about playing for anybody else.

Have faith in us, said Marina into my brain. *We're hustlers, ain't we? Just keep him occupied as best as you can.*

A'ight, I thought. *I'll do it. I'll do it.*

"I accept those terms," I said.

Right then the witch's bond appeared on my finger. It

burned it did, I wanted to holler out and cry it hurt so bad, but I didn't want to embarrass myself. For what it's worth, Boss Authority winced too, I saw it on his face.

"The bond is set," said Marina. "There ain't any other option now."

"Enough gabbing," I said. "Let's sit down already and play."

17

ON MY LEFT SAT DRUSILLA Fey, dainty as at a dinner party, and to my right Marina, still clutching her bare arm, glowering down like she was out for blood. I felt like no matter what happened between me and Boss Authority, the real battle was here, between witches, a grudge that went deeper and longer and fiercer than even I was aware of. The rest of them—Tally, Pop, Cecily Bob and Mr. Hugo, Lawrence and Johnson—gathered around us, watching, ready.

I sat there scared out of my mind, facing Boss Authority himself—muscled and tattooed and strange-eyed, magic running like little snakes in black lines through his skin. He would quiver and twitch with it, something sparking in him, like he'd sucked in so much power his skin could hardly contain it. I didn't know what a man had to go through to want something like that, all the power in the world, so much power it twisted him weird and raw. On his fingers glittered jewels set in bone, around his neck were strung pouches filled with the dust of organs and eyeballs, magic stuff, enchanted all of it, dirt from a thousand-year-old grave, dirty scraps from a bride's torn veil. He was a fearsome man, I knew that, his ponytail flickering through the air behind him, like it was ready to strike. I didn't even think he was in control of it all anymore, if there was even a Bobby Felix there left under all that gathered magic. He had hexed himself into something more than human, that's for sure, but he had lost something in the bargain, you could tell just by looking in that ruined eye of his.

"Stop gawking and shuffle," he said.

We exchanged decks, Boss Authority and me. I touched his and yanked my hand back. It was like the cards had moved, they had flinched under my touch, they were a living thing, like a spider or a rat. I was scared the sucker had teeth. Boss Authority sat there grinning at me.

It only then occurred to me just how outmatched I truly was.

What in the heck was I even doing? This was a terrible idea. I was gonna die, Pop was gonna die, Tally would probably die. Heck, the whole swamp would fall under the control of a maniac with a magic problem.

Well, it was too late now. Might as well make a good

show of it, go out with some kind of a bang.

The cards sailed through the air in a flurry, Boss Authority hardly even touching them as they scattered and mixed themselves. I had to do it the old-fashioned way, shuffling them same as I would any old deck. It was humiliating, it was, so I tried to do the accordion-thing. All the cards fell scattered on the table. Cecily Bob and Mr. Hugo busted out laughing. Even Drusilla Fey cracked a grin.

"Lawrence, I do believe we are doomed," said Johnson, trying to whisper.

This did not make me feel any better. And yet, as I scooped the cards up, there was Tally, lingering a little too close to the table. She put her hand on my shoulder and looked into my eyes.

"I believe in you," she said.

"Thanks," I whispered. "Glad somebody does."

I turned to my daddy, hunkered over in a chair, nursing his wounds. He looked red-eyed and drained, nothing but terror and a sort of manic worn-outness drawing wrinkles all over his face.

"Wish me luck?" I said.

Pop grinned at me. "Buddy, I thought you'd never ask."

He slipped the vine from around his neck and snapped it quiet in his palm.

I felt it then, the hex break. It was like someone dumping cold water onto me on a hot day, like running outside bare-chested in a snowstorm. It shivered me scalp to toes, it did. I felt like I'd had some kind of supernatural bath, like the stars and moon had finally come out in the great black sky of my life. I hadn't known how bad that hex had felt, it had been so long since I'd been usual. I had forgotten what being uncursed even felt like. For the first time since I was just a little kid, I finally felt like myself again.

It made me real mad at Pop, to be honest with you. No, not mad. That ain't the right word at all. Bitter is how it made me feel, just a little bit, that I had suffered all that time and it was his doing. Pop knew it, too, I could tell, the way he hunkered back down in his chair and wouldn't hardly look at me.

"Someone's let a piece of magic loose in here," said Drusilla Fey. "An old hex has been broken, I can smell it for miles. They're cheating, they are. You want me to call it off, Boss?"

"Let them cheat," he said. "Might at least make this duel interesting." He looked at me, his weird eye turning loops in his head. "Go ahead then, Buddy boy. Draw."

This was it then. I shut my eyes and said a prayer.

Please let it be the Fish Boy. Please oh please let it be the Fish Boy.

I drew my card and flipped it over and there he was. The awkward kid, a little slouched, his hair all mussed and wild, his eyes full with wonder—more and more like me he looked, more even than back on the skiff—holding a little wooden cup in his hands, that big old catfish half leaping out, whiskers flaring, as if he'd popped up to ask a question.

I'd gotten this far before, sure, but it was still a relief to do it when it really mattered. I'd drawn the Fish Boy. *My* card, more than any other card was mine. That was a start, it was.

Boss Authority just sat across from me and smiled, that blank eye of his boring right down into my soul it felt like, seeing into the deeps of me, into my stomach and heart and bones. It was like I could feel him, crawling through my skin, poking at my dreams and desires. Like he was knowing me, Boss Authority was, seeing all kinds of stuff he had no right to.

I felt a burning feeling right in the back of my head, and Boss Authority flinched a little.

"Keep your eye on yourself," hissed Marina.

I nodded her a thank-you, but I don't think she noticed.

I Orated then. It wasn't the same thing I told Radegar, but it was close. About how this Fish Boy never fit in anywhere, about how all he wanted to do was be somewhere else, back to the river, back to anywhere, and his hope was always that this magic catfish could lead him home, to where he belonged. That it would lead him back to his daddy.

By the end of my talking, I realized the catfish had only one eye on his head, right there in the center. Now that was something.

"My magic, that is," said Drusilla Fey. "That was me plucking the strings of fate, trying to call all Boss's possessions back to him."

"You're the one who sent all them one-eyed creatures at me?" I said. "Even the toad that mesmerized me and got my mom's bakery all burned down?"

She laughed, a high shrieking thing, and a weird eye sprouted in her forehead, all horizontal-like, and blinked three times. Then it sank bank into her noggin like it never was there at all.

"I sent out a call to gather back into the swamp all things that were owed to Boss Authority," she said. "And here you came!"

"But why?" I said. "You could have called Pop to you whenever you wanted. Why now?"

"I'll tell you why she waited," said Marina. "He wasn't strong enough. That's the truth of the matter. Sure, he had the power to lock me up in this house, but that was just because of your stupid daddy over there. One on one, Bobby Felix couldn't take me, not even with his pet witch here at his side. Same with Baudelaire Quatro. His was the last Parsnit house standing, Bobby Felix had made good and sure of that, but he didn't have the power in him to burn it to the ground. It's only now, after he's hoarded those piddly little enchantments of his, after he's cheated and swindled and flat bullied the magic out of every witch and mystic and Parsnit player this side of the river, did he have it in him to try and take over the swamp. That's why he waited, Buddy. He was too durn weak."

Boss Authority slammed his fist down on the table so hard I thought it'd crack.

"Yeah, I wasn't strong enough, yeah I was weak!" he roared. "But that ain't all it was. No, sir, that ain't the half of it." He pointed his big metal finger up at Pop. "It was him! I wanted him to see it! I wanted Davey Boy to see me in my glory, to watch as I took all that was once his and made it mine. I wanted to see Davey Boy humiliated. So I had Drusilla Fey cast her spell upon the waters, to call back to me all I'd won. You wouldn't believe the riffraff that's been floating up to my shores, all the scoundrels swirling in the muck."

Boss Authority turned his weird eye on me in a stare so hard I could feel it, like something invisible in him reached right out and grabbed me by the collar.

"But Buddy boy," said Boss Authority, "I tell you what. Of all the things that came drifting my way, you are the prize piece. Your blood will be the trophy I wear around my neck for the rest of my life. That and the beautiful look of terror on your daddy's face while he watches me drain it right out of you."

Oh boy, not a thing on this earth could have made me madder than that. But I had to stuff that anger down deep. It wouldn't do to get furious, not quite yet. I still had a Parsnit duel to win.

"Your play, Boss," I said.

Boss flipped his card next. I figured it would be something mighty, like Old Redbeard or King One Eye or even the Hobble Mystic. Some card to strike fear in me, some warlord card to pummel my little Fish Boy to smithereens.

But nope, Boss Authority flipped the Fish Boy, same as me. Except of course his Fish Boy looked a little different. The kid was shorter than mine, squatter too, like God took a normal-sized kid and squished him down a little with His thumb. He had sandy hair and zits all over his face, and he stood in a messy kitchen with pots and pans tossed all over the floor, spilling stinking-looking food everywhere.

And Boss Authority began to Orate.

As he spoke, his voice lost its snarl, it lost all the meanness and grit. It got softer, it did, gentler. Boss Authority was speaking like a normal person, like a kid even. I looked back at my daddy and I could see it right there, in all the anguish on his face, like he was remembering something that gave him pain all over. Boss Authority wasn't talking like a Boss anymore. No, he was little Bobby Felix all over again.

He spoke of a lonesome home, of a wretched mom and a no-account daddy. He spoke of holes in the floor and rats in his bed. He spoke of waking up in the night to a snake trying to swallow a bat, a fight to the death right in the corner of the room.

I saw the card begin to shimmer and glow as Boss told the story of it. I realized then that I could smell the food on his table, rotten and putrid, that I could hear the flies buzzing all around it. These cards were powerful, they were. The Fish Boy held not a goblet or a cup but a big metal pot, and rising up from it was an alligator gar, long-snouted, fang-toothed, and ornery. It was coming for the Fish Boy, it was. It looked like it was about to bite his nose off.

It made me feel bad for Boss Authority's Fish Boy, like there was nothing that kid could ever do right, like every time he tried it all just went wrong for him. You could feel his loneliness right then and there, in your bones, you could feel the big empty deep in your own heart.

I guess what I mean is I could relate to that Fish Boy, I really could. I knew all about loneliness, about having nobody to talk to, nobody to play with, everybody running off and hiding whenever you take a walk outside. My whole life in Collardsville had been just the same way. Boss

Authority's card told the truth, it did, and maybe I related to it even more than I did my own.

I shook it off. It was time for me to flip another card, my Home card.

I remembered my last failure at Baudelaire Quatro's, where all I did was embarrass myself. Here the penalty would be much more severe. I didn't even want to think about that, if you want the honest truth. I was sweating so bad my shirt was drenched through and I thought my heart was going to beat out of my chest. I reached my hand toward the deck and it was shaking so bad I couldn't hardly get hold of a card.

In my mind I wanted the Staggerly Road, the meanest, snarliest patch of earth you ever dreamed of, something easy for the Fish Boy to be heroic on. Or maybe the Wayward River, nothing but the rambling life for this kid, his true home not some wooden shack somewhere but the wild free air under the bright and roving stars, be it land or water or any other kind of world the Good Lord created. That's the Home card for this Fish Boy, I'm telling you what.

But neither of those were the cards I drew. No sir.

My first card was the Bone Queen, definitely not a Home card. Next was the most durn useless card in the whole deck, the Bilious Chef, holding his swollen belly. No Home card there either.

I flipped the top card and laid it down.

But my third card most certainly was a Home card. I'd done it.

Yes sir, I'd gotten further now than I had with Radegar, and I was surely grateful for that. When I laid it down on the table I heard Tally let out a big relieved sigh next to me, and it didn't even bother me any, I was so glad I hadn't just doomed us all. I started to feel a little better, I did. Not good, mind you. Just better, like it wasn't all lost yet, like there might be some hope out there after all.

Except guess what Home card I drew? Not the Wayward River, no sir, a card I could talk for days and days on end about. Not the Far Yonder Mountains neither, not the Staggerly Road, which was something I could cast some dreams on. I did not even draw the durn Bramble. You know what card I turned?

The Sleepy Town.

Yep, that's right, the single most boring card there is. It's a morning sunrise, a tumbleweed rolling down a road, maybe a drowsy dog yawning in the early light. Just a bunch of buildings, maybe one with some smoke in the chimney, a tall brick place like what Mom's bakery should have been. You know what else is going on in the Sleepy Town? Nothing. I mean it. Even the dog looks bored to tears. That couldn't be my Fish Boy's Home card, no way no how. But that's the card I flipped and there was nothing else for me to do except Orate it as good and wild as I could.

I took a deep breath and got to it.

"Fish Boy's waking up in Sleepy Town, he is, up even before the rooster crows, up before there's anything except a big-eared dog lazing around. Yes sir, the Fish Boy is wide-awake, and he has been for hours."

I could see it, the Sleepy Town forming out of the haze in my mind—Collardsville, in all its sad boring glory. But the more I began to talk about it, the more it started to matter to me. I remembered what it was like, waking up those early mornings, wishing I was somewhere else. Wishing I was on an adventure.

"You wanna know why that Fish Boy's awake?" I said. "I'll tell you why. He's been daydreaming. He's been daydreaming of this wild world he knows exists out there, far beyond the town. The world he was born into, a world of magic and action, a world of chance, of gamblers and knife fights, the roving roaming world, yes sir, that's the world he's dreaming of. But dreaming don't get him there, not even close. Dreaming ain't good for much of anything."

The Sleepy Town seemed to flicker and vanish in the air, and then it was gone. My first round of Orating was over.

Okay, so I hadn't exactly done great, but at least it was.

a start. The tension in the room relaxed a little bit, like it wasn't just me who was relieved. I could Orate, I knew that now. Me and the cards were working up the beginnings of a story.

Out of the corner of my eye I saw Harlen the dog-man crouched low, his beard scraping the floor, all tense, ready to move. Then he leapt out Marina's side window, busting right through the glass. Drusilla Fey was up from her chair in a second, hollering hexes hard as she could through the night.

"I'll send rabid bats after him," she said. "I'll call down lightning to fall, won't be more than a smudge of the beast left."

"No you will not," said Boss Authority. "I need your magic here, Drusilla. I need your attention on the duel, especially with this one sitting witch next to you." He pointed a metal finger at Marina, who sat with a fierce grin on her face, like she'd just gotten away with something. See, I knew everyone was hustling, I knew everyone was up to something, especially Marina. I just didn't know exactly what it was yet.

"Want me after him, Boss?" said Cecily Bob.

"Let the man-dog go," said Boss Authority. "He don't concern me."

"I don't like it, Boss," said Drusilla Fey.

"If I ever give one hoot about what you like or don't like," said Boss Authority, "I shall kindly let you know."

She stuck her tongue out at him and hissed. Boss Authority chuckled, his clockwork fist creaking like an old rusty door hinge.

"Still, perhaps y'all are right," said Boss Authority. "Maybe you better track that dog-fella, Cecily Bob, if you can manage it."

Cecily Bob nodded at Boss. "I'm on it," he said, and walked on out the front door. I saw Pop relax a little, now that only one set of knives was on him.

Boss Authority popped his iron knuckles and drew his Home cards and threw down the Night Shack.

In Pop's deck, the Night Shack was some kind of clubhouse hidden off in the woods, and there was a fire burning and you could see folks dancing in the windows, light gleaming bright and casting its glow on the dark night outside. It was a happy place, Pop's Night Shack was, a place of joy and contentment, like your own special hiding place where you can do whatever you want and feel secret about it. You know that feeling? It's one of the best there is, at least in my estimation of things. It's how I felt every time I held that card in my hand and studied it, that adventure feeling.

Well, listen here. Boss Authority's Night Shack wasn't anything like that. For one, the place was wrecked, with a big hole in the roof, a porch that sagged, and a railing that fell in, and all the windows busted. The house was dark, and coyotes roamed outside of it, howling at the cruel Heaven stars. And peeking out the window was the saddest little kid face you ever saw in your whole life.

"That Fish Boy never belonged at home," said Boss Authority. "He never belonged anywhere. He'd sit up at night waiting, waiting, hoping someone would come home for him. And they never did."

It went on like that, on and on. And the thing was, the more Boss Authority talked, the more I felt it. How that was me growing up, staring out the window at night, hoping Pop would come for me. That was me, night after night, way into the deepest darkest moonless nights, waiting and praying and hoping, and none of those prayers or hopes coming true. I felt so lonely, I did, my bones ached with it, my little kid heart just broke over and over and over again.

I was crying, I was. Right there at the Parsnit table, in front of Pop and Tally and everyone else. But I wasn't crying for Boss Authority, I was crying for me.

And that's when I understood what true Orating was. It isn't just about telling your own story. It's about telling your story in a way that makes it someone else's story too, maybe even more theirs than yours when the telling's all over. It's inviting someone else into the tale and letting them live there awhile, letting them put their own hearts and feelings and lives into it, and then saying, *Here, you can keep it, it's yours now.* That's what Boss Authority did every time he opened his mouth. His words might as well have been mine. They would have been mine too, if I was half the Orator he was.

Truth be told, Boss Authority was whooping my tail right now. I didn't stand one ghost of a chance of winning this one, unless I got lucky, and fast. Good thing I had half Pop's blood running through me, the luckiest blood in the whole Swamplands.

Now came the time for us to lay down Journey cards against each other. I drew the first card and held it tight in my hands. It was a good card, but one that wasn't quite so powerful for me this time around, how I was feeling right now. I drew the Rambling Duke.

I laid the Rambling Duke faceup, the tall gangly traveler with a knapsack full of cards, a swagger to his steps, a gold tooth glimmering in his mouth. I played the card of my pop, charged with all the love and power I could muster, and I thrust it at Boss Authority, trying to figure how on earth he could overpower a card so full of love as that one.

But Boss Authority just grinned at me, this weird trickster's grin, like he'd set this trap for me ages and ages ago and I'd just blundered myself right into it. Scared me, it did, shivered me right through my bones. I didn't know what all was about to happen to me.

"Let me tell you the story of how the Fish Boy met his

hero," said Boss Authority. "When the Fish Boy was a little older, say seventeen or so, he ran away from home, he did, left his wretched lying mom and his evil-tempered daddy and took off to the swamp. Why the swamp? Because nobody knew him there. Because it was a place his mom never went and his daddy was scared of. Because it was the only place left in this whole wide world where he would be safe from the both of them, where nobody had ever heard of him or his family, where he could make himself new. Besides, a swamp wasn't so bad, was it? It was beautiful in the mornings, when the sun cut through the trees and burned all the water gold. The cattails swaying in the wind, the dew on a spiderweb, the dragonflies and hummingbirds, the turtles that rose and vanished at their whims, snakes long and glistening on the water. It was all beautiful, astonishing, and new every day. Even now he remembers rowing out on his first clear night in the swamp, a big bright moon thick and gold and juicy as a peach up there, and seeing all the stars reflected in the water beneath him, like he was drifting through them, a tiny canoe that had left the old world and cut a path through space. He knew this would be the place for him, this would be where he could become someone new, the person he secretly was, the person he'd always wanted to be."

Boss Authority was up to something, and I didn't like it. So far his story was better than mine, and that was a fact. I was hoping whatever card he played against me next gave me more to work with than the Sleepy Town had.

Boss Authority drew his Journey card and plopped the Dolly Witch down on the table.

The Dolly Witch? What was I supposed to say about her?

I took a close look at that card, searching for clues. Because his Dolly Witch was different than Pop's. In fact, there was something awful familiar about the witch on this card. The black hair, no speck of gray, the eyes light and silver. The smile that always looked like it was hiding something, like it was two steps ahead of you. And then it hit me. That was my mom there, that Dolly Witch, just younger, a lot younger, like how she was when she and Pop first met. Boss Authority's Dolly Witch was my mom.

Okay. I could say a little something about the Dolly Witch. I could say something about my mom. I shut my eyes and gave it my best.

"Every morning the Fish Boy wakes up right at dawn," I said, "because he's got himself some chores to do. His mom, she runs that bakery you see right there on the Sleepy Town card, the one chimney puffing smoke. You know why it's puffing smoke so early in the morning? Because the Fish Boy was up to get the fires going, he was, that was his number one job. A baker in a small town has to hustle same as everybody else, maybe even harder. Folks can make their own bread, can they not? But there's something special about his mom's cooking, and he knows it. There's something extra in it. It ain't quite occurred to him yet that it's magic in that bread, it's magic in those pastries and pies, that it's big heart magic that makes all that food worth eating, that makes even poor families shell out an extra coin or two just for a taste. His mom bakes it all, all by herself. Sure, the Fish Boy helps where he can, but nothing ever quite goes right if he helps too much. The bread gets burned, or the dough doesn't rise, or maybe a soufflé just flattens itself right then and there. No, he does what he can, cleaning and chopping wood and feeding the fire, but it's his mom that does all the work. Morning till sunset, his mom, working harder than anyone ever worked in their whole life, trying to make a living, trying to make a good world for her boy. For her Fish Boy."

I didn't know what was coming over me. I saw Mom, hands calloused and burned, little scars on her arms, shoving dough in the ovens so hot you got to squint when you're near them. I saw Mom bone-tired and lonely every night, asleep before she even gets her boots off. Mom with no friends, Mom hurt and lonesome, Mom missing Pop, crying about it when she thought I wasn't looking. I never understood it until I tried to tell the story. I never understood just how hard her life was, just how lonely.

Right then a memory came to my mind, a strange one, and painful, and I knew it was mine to Orate.

The memory was of a time when a carnival came to town.

Maybe "carnival" makes it sound bigger than it was. Really a few horse-drawn wagons with a handful of clowns showed up. Still, it was a pretty big deal in Collardsville, and everybody flocked out into the streets to see them. Me and Mom were working in the bakery (she had me sweeping and dusting at the time, because at least I could sweep up okay without ruining everything) when Mom grabbed me by the hand and yanked me outside.

"But I'm not finished yet," I said. "You told me I have to be done before dinner, and at this rate, I won't ever eat."

And she said, "Are you kidding me, Buddy? We got us a carnival in town."

I don't know why, but I was feeling pretty crummy that day. I didn't want to see any two-bit carnival, with no fire-breathers or elephants or sword-swallowers or tigers or even a big tent to its name. But Mom seemed so excited about the whole thing, so thrilled at the prospect of something new, that I let her yank me right out the door and into the streets of Collardsville.

The carnival wagons were something else, I'll tell you. They were big canvas things with strange symbols painted on them—a cardinal and an eyeball, a giant fishhook, a candle burning at both ends. The clowns had a darkness to them too, a strangeness to their makeup—all drawn-on right angles and jagged lines and gray colors—and they slunk around all seedy and dangerous-looking, not a bit funny.

Needless to say, I liked them already.

They began stumbling around in a circle, spinning slowly at first, then faster, and faster. It was like watching a whirlpool open up in the empty field in front of us, like any moment we would all spiral down into blackness.

Suddenly they all stopped at once, and they stood so still it was like time itself stopped, like the sand had frozen in every hourglass in the village. One of the clowns—the tallest one, with sloped shoulders and long gangly legs—cupped a hand to his ear, and leaned into the wind, like he was listening real close for something. After a moment he began to sing.

It was a high and mournful song, something that could be belted out across the Long Lonely Prairie, or would echo down from the tallest tower of the Old Crumbly Castle. It was a magic song, full of longing for things long gone, for a home abandoned. It was an exile's song, it was, a wish for escape, for adventure, for any life but the life you were living.

The clown finished and all was still and quiet, not even a dog barked in the street. The clown opened his hand and in his palm was a rose, a long thorny one, so bloodred it seemed to be dripping. He offered the rose to my mom. I looked in her eyes, and I saw something I hadn't seen in ages. It was like the furnaces of the bakery were burning bright in them, like in that moment my mom was capable of anything. There was possibility in her eyes.

But then the moment seemed to pass from her, and her eyes sparkled instead of burned, and she took the rose and laughed. The clown did a backflip, and the wagon unveiled a troupe of musicians who began bashing and strumming away. And we all danced together, Mom even got me to dance, and we laughed and spun and hollered. I gripped Mom's rose in my teeth and she twirled me. I couldn't remember a time since Pop left that was so much fun.

When we left the carnival, it was nearing dusklight. I was about as happy as I'd ever felt in my whole life. I mean, I was practically skipping, dancing around Mom, and neither of us could go five seconds without laughing.

Then I had to go and screw it all up. I had to open my durn stupid mouth.

I looked up at my mom, her face so beaming and glad and full of joy it might have been the moon itself.

I said, "Man, Pop would have really loved that, wouldn't he?"

The light went quick out of her face, same as a candle being snuffed out.

Mom stopped in her tracks and hung her head a minute. I saw her neck flinch, and her right hand make a fist, like she was holding something in, like she was doing everything she could not to rear back and scream.

When she finally spoke, it was in a whisper.

"There are only so many stories that get told," she said.

"I don't understand," I said. "Are you talking about that song the clown sang?"

"It's like in Parsnit," said Mom. "You know how the best stories are all about the Rambling Duke, or the Mountebank, or any old adventurer who takes off down the Wayward River?"

"Yeah," I said. "So?"

"There are other stories, Buddy," she said. "Of folks who maybe aren't quite so free, who can't just pack up and run after any adventure that comes their way. Their stories might not seem as exciting, and they might take place somewhere regular and boring. But that doesn't mean these folks haven't sacrificed and loved and lost and fought battles just as hard as someone out on the road. It doesn't make their stories any less powerful, important, or real. It doesn't make their stories mean any less."

"I don't get it," I said. "How can the story about someone who doesn't go on an adventure be as interesting as a story about someone who does?"

Mom smiled at me, but it was a sad smile, and all the sparkle was gone out from her eyes.

"Come on home now," she said. "We got an early morning tomorrow."

And we walked the rest of the way in silence.

It was only now, thinking back to the way my mom's eyes

flashed and burned for a moment, that I realized all she had given up for me. That maybe she didn't want a quiet home life, that maybe her heart longed for wildness, for adventure. I mean, why else would she have taken up with a guy like Pop in the first place? And yet all she got out of the deal was to be stuck at home, with me.

With me, who could only ever think of Pop.

That was more or less the way I told it, but like it was happening to the Fish Boy instead of to me. The room was silent when I finished. Then I heard a little crying sound coming from behind me. I turned and looked. It was Pop crying. It was Pop crying at my Orating, knowing good and well I was telling the story of his strong powerful lonely wife he abandoned. Spooked me, it did. I never saw my daddy cry before.

Drusilla Fey sat smirking at me, but nobody else thought it was funny. Even Boss Authority wasn't laughing. He seemed hurt, like maybe he knew some of what I was talking about, what hard work and loneliness were. Like maybe Boss Authority understood a little bit.

"Durn fine Orating!" said Lawrence, clacking the ground with his cane.

"Hear hear!" said Johnson.

But Boss Authority just sat there, grinning that mysterious

awful grin of his. I didn't like it. I didn't like it one bit.

"Buddy," he said, calm as could be, "how about you go ahead and throw down that Dolly Witch card you're about to draw next?"

"What?" I said.

"You heard me," he said. "Your next card is the Dolly Witch, so go ahead and draw it. It's time for her in this story anyhow."

I reached my hand out and flipped the top card of my deck. There she was, the Dolly Witch, gray-headed and tired, but with a power in her eyes. I saw it now, how much she looked like my mom. I didn't know how Boss Authority knew I had the Dolly Witch coming, and it spooked me. I didn't know what else he knew about my cards that I didn't.

"Soon enough the Fish Boy made friends," said Boss Authority. "Specifically, one friend. She was a witch, she was, the prettiest witch in the whole swamp. Better than that, she was nice to him. A good person through and through, and kind. The Fish Boy knew she was only nice to him because he was strange and friendless, that maybe she only took pity on him. But that was fine. Nobody had ever taken pity on the Fish Boy before, and pity was preferable to anything else he'd yet experienced."

Boss Authority took a deep breath and let it out slow, his eyes crinkled shut, like the next part of the story was hard to tell, like it hurt him too bad to say it.

"But of course, this kindly witch had herself a man. The Rambling Duke, he was, and there wasn't a handsomer fella in the whole swamp. Immediately he became the Fish Boy's hero. I mean, his absolute idol. It never occurred to the Fish Boy to be jealous of the Rambling Duke, no sir. There wasn't any question in his mind that he could compete with someone like the Duke, someone so wild and charming, someone with such natural luck, who could stumble through any situation and come out rich. Naw, the Fish Boy wasn't jealous of the Rambling Duke. He loved the witch and he loved her man, and it was enough for him to be around them, for them to pay attention to him. They brought him along with them, let the Fish Boy join their little group, even gave him some responsibility, put him in charge of a job here and there. It was the proudest the Fish Boy had ever been in himself, the happiest too. He'd finally found a place for himself, and something like a family."

I could feel it, yes sir, the warmth of love, of belonging somewhere, of having friends like I'd always dreamed of. Because that had been my wish this whole time. To find a place for myself, to quit being a failure and a mess-up, to take up where my daddy left off. To be a part of a family again. That's what I'd wanted all along, same as Boss Authority's Fish Boy.

Boss Authority opened his eyes wide then, the white one gone strange, sort of a churning whirlpool in it, milky and swirling. He turned his head and stared my daddy down, that ponytail of his lifting high like a snake about to strike. A meanness crept back in his voice right then, all grit and thorns.

"And then came the worst night of the Fish Boy's life," said Boss Authority. "The night when he learned the true nature of his new friends."

"Please," said Pop, his voice a whisper. "Please don't tell this part. Not in front of my boy."

"Oh, I fully intend to," said Boss Authority. "I intend to tell your boy every single word of it."

"I'm begging you," said Pop.

That's when Marina cut in. "You don't have the right, David. You don't have the right to tell Bobby Felix what he can and can't say." She cast her eyes down to the table. "No matter how bad it hurts."

Drusilla Fey licked her lips and giggled a little bit, like she was enjoying all this pain and strangeness. I myself had not one clue what was about to happen, what kind of story it was Boss Authority was going to tell. I was pretty sure this had nothing to do with Parsnit though, that it had everything to do with real life, something my daddy had done to Boss long ago.

"See, now this Fish Boy was learning a little something about himself," said Boss. "He wasn't any witch, mind you, but he had a spark to his blood, a shiver of magic in his bones. Nothing much, but a little. And that little was the most of anything all his own that he'd ever had. So he cultivated it, he made it grow. He read and he studied, and he learned. It was slow going, sure, book by book, scroll by scroll, herb by herb. In time he realized he had a gift with plants, with making green things sprout and bloom. He could conjure near anything healthy and whole out of the muck of the swamp, make it blossom into a thousand swirling colors, a whole sunset of flowers let loose in his palms. That's right, his early gift was beauty, this ugly guppy of a Fish Boy, weaker and smaller and tinier than all the rest. He could make pretty things bloom.

"He just wanted to thank her, is all," said Boss Authority, his voice cracking a little. "He just wanted to make something lovely for her, to thank her for giving him a home, a place, even friends, or what he thought were friends. He could do that much. So he grew her a painting. He planted his seeds and spun his magic, the vines sprouting and looping around a wooden picture frame he'd made, a little trellis on the inside to hold it all together. It took him months, maybe even a year, to get the colors right, to make the plants blossom and bloom just so. But he did it, he grew her a picture, a portrait, and it was beautiful. It looked just like her, the way the light would catch her in the early morning, when the sunrise made the whole swamp new, in the best moments of the day, before anything had happened, when all was still possible. That's how this Fish Boy grew a present for the Dolly Witch.

"He didn't think he had a chance with her, no sir. He wasn't even in love, not like that. It was just a thank-you, something beautiful to give, because words weren't always his strong suit. Still, he was a little scared, about what the Rambling Duke might think. So he picked a time when the Duke and his cronies would be off somewhere, pulling a job they didn't bother to invite him along to, they didn't even think he knew about. And the Fish Boy went over to the witch's house, to bring her a present. It was just around moonrise, as I recall, and the fireflies were aglow all over the swamp. I felt like I was floating past the stars and planets, I did, walking to her place. I felt like I had left this world and found myself somewhere better."

Boss Authority wasn't even Orating anymore, not really. He was telling me a story, I realized, a true one. But the power of the cards remained, and I could see him, the Fish Boy, a little runt of a fella with a pug face, carrying this giant portrait of flowers. I could smell them, they smelled like honey and lavender, they smelled like Mom's bakery in the afternoon, with the pies just out of the oven. I was walking with him, I was, not even the Fish Boy, but Boss Authority when he was younger, just barely an adult. I could feel the joy and anticipation sparking in his heart, how excited he was to give the witch his present, to thank her for being so kind to him. I couldn't wait to give it to her either. It was all I wanted in the world.

"Bobby Felix," said Pop. "Please."

Again Boss Authority slammed his clockwork fist on the table, this time splintering it.

"Don't you talk," he said. "Don't you say another word. This is my story, and I'm telling it exactly as it happened."

There was a moment of stillness then, a flicker of magic thick as fog in the air, you could smell it, you could taste it. Everyone was rapt, no one moved. Except for Tally, inching along toward Boss Authority, her hands in her pockets, just a trace of spider on her face. What was Tally up to?

But I couldn't think about it for long, because Boss Authority got back to his tale, and the magic swallowed me whole.

"I tell you again," said Boss Authority, "I had no designs on her. I only wanted to say thank you. And when I opened that door, expecting to see Samantha Annie's face beaming at me, all smiling at the pretty little thing I grew her, I was about the happiest man on this earth, and that's a fact."

I saw her then, my mom as she was when she was young. Bright and pretty and strong, unafraid. None of the scars from the oven or the crow's-feet around her eyes, no hint of worry or exhaustion or frustration. I saw her the way Boss

Authority saw her, just the same as she was on his Parsnit card, and she was beautiful.

"But when I opened that door, who should I see there but the Rambling Duke himself, old Davey Boy Pennington, and his durn cronies. Awful Sinclair, that durned redneck pretty boy, and a couple others. All sitting around, laughing at their bad jokes, mugs half-empty, lousing up the place.

"'What do we got here?' said Davey Boy. 'Looks like Bobby Felix got himself a picture. It's a pretty picture, ain't it boys?'

"'Y'all ain't supposed to be here,' I said. 'Y'all are supposed to be gone.'

"'But we ain't, are we, boys?' he said. 'Nope, we're right here. Right where you are.'

"'If I ain't mistaken,' said Sinclair, the louse, the coward, 'that there flower picture looks an awful lot like your girlfriend, don't it, Davey?'

"'Sir, I do believe you're right. How do you feel about it, Sinclair?'

"'I believe the runt has his sights set on your lady, I do.'

"'She isn't your lady,' I said. 'She's her own, and she's my friend.'

"'Your friend is she?' said Davey Boy. 'I suppose that's right. She's the only reason we keep you around, anyway. But I'm starting to think you've overstayed your welcome, Bobby Felix.'

"'But this is my home,' I said. 'The only place I ever belonged.'

"'Belonged?' said Davey Boy. 'You'll never belong here. Not with us.'

"Davey Boy started to dance, a stupid little jig, singing while the others clapped. And he took my flowers and he shredded them, he plucked them out one by one and scattered them across the floor. I scrambled to pick them up, my months of work, all my heart put into that, and they began pushing me, back and forth, spinning me around until I got dizzy, until I thought I'd vomit. Then they picked me up by my trousers, they did, and tossed me back and forth, little guppy that I was, little runt. That's what my daddy always called me, Runt, or Worm, or Scab, anything nasty he could.

"'You hang on to her like a scab,' said your daddy. 'Like a tick, sucking her blood. And I won't have it anymore. I won't have you anymore.'

"My shirt ripped first, my best shirt, the one I saved up all my money for. That went straight to the floor, with my wilting ruined flowers. Sinclair shoved me hard as he could and I tripped, I fell face-forward, and your daddy yanked me by the back of my trousers. And as I fell, they ripped. I mean, clean split down to my ankles.

"I tumbled naked onto the floor of Samantha Annie's cabin.

"And that's when the door opened. There stood Samantha Annie, with her witch pal Marina right behind her, staring aghast at me, naked and dirty and weeping, covered in browning rose petals, while the rest of them stood around and laughed. I bolted past her and threw myself into the swamp, into the mud and snakes and leeches, into the scum of it all. And that's where I been ever since."

I could feel it, oh the emptiness and despair, the pain and humiliation that cuts inside of you, that rots you from your bones. I'd never felt a thing like it. I'd never felt so lonely and awful in all my life.

The room was silent, then, entirely, nary even the buzzing of a mosquito. I couldn't believe it, my daddy acting that way. Pop, who was my hero, my favorite person in all the world, the man I'd always wanted to be like, who I'd wanted to imitate down to the gold tooth in his mouth ever since I could remember. Pop, who I came all this way for.

"So now, little fella, you know your pop, who he really is," said Boss Authority. "But didn't you know all along? Wasn't it he who left you and your mom to fend for yourselves in that godforsaken town up north? Wasn't it he who only showed up every year or two, who never bothered to know you, who never bothered enough to be a real daddy? He whose arrogance doomed you, who was so cocky he could not conceive of losing to a little runt like me, that he was willing to bet not only his blood, but yours as well? Who sold you out in a card game? Didn't you already know he was a scoundrel, a weasel, the worst kind of coward? Haven't you known it all along?"

Boss Authority laid down a Journey card then, his own Rambling Duke. He looked just like my daddy, he did, same gold tooth, same cocky grin on his face. But on Boss Authority's card, there was something ghastly to him too. The swagger was all menace, a bully on the prowl, his smile cruel, his eyes glistering with hatred. Blood all over his hands. This Rambling Duke was nothing but a villain, a swine, and a braggart, a dog of the lowest sort. But it was Pop all right, right there in front of me, like the card had flipped him inside out and shown me only his heart, how he really was.

"So tell your tale, boy," said Boss Authority. "Tell the story of the daddy who betrayed you, the father who let you down, the husband who abandoned his wife, the man who had everything and let it all ride on a game of cards. Tell it to me and tell it to yourself and tell it to everyone in this room. But most importantly, tell it to him, right over there." And he pointed with his long metal clockwork finger at my daddy, at Pop, weeping there in the corner.

"I'm so sorry, Buddy," said Pop. "I'm so, so sorry for everything."

Pop couldn't even look at me. He wouldn't dare even raise his eyes to mine. Pop was broken, and Boss Authority had used me to do it.

"No," I said. "That ain't my story. That's not how it goes at all."

But I was lying. That's the story the cards told now. I couldn't say another thing about it.

"Well then, if you got nothing further to add, why don't you go ahead and play your next card, Buddy," said Boss Authority. "Play the card that comes natural to this story, the only conclusion that's fair for the old Fish Boy, play the card of justice."

I flipped it over then. She stood cruel and menacing, three eyes on her head, one dead center, clad in ghastly crimson, a long black mark burned through her. The Red Bride, the revenge card. Boss Authority tipped his head backward and let out a cackle.

"There she is, Buddy," he said. "There's my justice. There's the recompense for all the misery your pop put me through."

And I guessed Pop deserved it, he did. There was nothing in me that could defend what Pop had done, not to Bobby Felix, not to Mom, not to me. Pop was a scoundrel, through and through, this man I had so admired, my own hero, same as he had been Bobby Felix's.

"You know what card comes next, don't you?" said Boss

Authority. "You know what card I'm going to turn and play against you. It's the Red Bride, same as what you played against me. It's the revenge card, it is. It's justice for the way your daddy's treated you and your mom. It's your revenge on all he's put you through, all the pain and loneliness, the way you had to leave your swamp home, for shutting y'all up in that awful village. It's what he deserves. So take this card and play it against your pop. Tell him just exactly how it is you feel. Tell him how much you hate his guts, how you're gonna smile while I drain him dry. You Orate it well enough, it might even save your life. I might even let your own blood stay right where it is, in your veins. I might not even squash that little spider-girl you made friends with. I might let her go free. How about it, Buddy? How will you tell the Red Bride what your pop has done?"

Boss Authority flipped the top card on his deck, that clockwork hand grinding, metal on metal, and laid it faceup on the table.

But no, it wasn't the Red Bride, not one bit. It was the Banquet Table. A long wooden table stuffed with food, folks lounging all around, laughing, breaking bread together. It was the table of friendship, of forgiveness. That's the card Boss laid down, not the Red Bride.

You should have seen his face. You should have seen that white swirly eye nearly pop right out of his skull.

"No," he said. "That ain't right. The Red Bride was next. I could feel her." He turned to Drusilla Fey. "What's happening here? What went wrong?"

Marina glared at him, her face stern as stone.

"That's the card you turned, Bobby," she said. "That's the card you got to play."

I looked over at my pop, huddling on the floor, moaning like a kicked dog. Boss Authority was right, I was awful mad at him. I was ashamed of him. The pain I felt in my guts was deep, and it had changed everything for me, probably forever. But I also realized something else, right there in that moment, watching him curled up on the floor crying.

Pop had hurt me worse than anyone ever had, and that was a fact. But all the same, I realized I still loved Pop. No matter what he had done, no matter what he would do. I loved my pop, and only people you love can hurt you like that. That's why Mom sat up nights crying, that's why she wouldn't let Pop into the house when he came by to visit. It's because she still loved him, and that's what made it hurt so much. I still loved Pop too. Maybe that's wrong, or maybe that's what love is, how it's unconditional, how it forgives and forgives. I'm not saying it forgets, because never could I forget what I had seen and felt from Boss Authority's Orating, never could I forget the cruelness on my daddy's face, never could I forget how it felt to be the object of a losing wager. It all mattered, it did, and nothing would ever be the same. Pop wasn't my hero anymore, not by a long shot. When I grew up, I didn't want to be anything like him, not anymore. I wanted to be someone better, someone kinder and gentler, someone who would never bully or hurt another person, someone who would never take my family for granted. But even if he wasn't perfect, if sometimes he was downright wicked, I still loved my pop. And I realized I always would.

"Fine, Boss," I said. "I'll tell my tale. I'll tell the story of the Fish Boy who loved the Rambling Duke so much until he found out he wasn't perfect, that he'd done some downright horrible things in his life. Oh and it broke that little boy's heart, it did. And Boss, I want to apologize to you, on behalf of my daddy, who ruined your life. I know it ain't any consolation—nothing could ever be, not really—but you didn't deserve that, not one bit. And if my blood has any say in the matter, then let my apology count for something. Please."

I bowed my head to him.

"But if you think what Pop did gives you the right to bully other people, to rob them and steal from them and banish them, to take power over other folks any way you see fit, well, you're just wrong about that. And I won't stand for it. Because let me tell you something about this Fish Boy right here. He still loves his pop, flawed a man as he is, and this boy still forgives his daddy for every ounce of pain he caused him. Let me tell you, Boss, forgiveness can whoop vengeance's tail anytime.

"Besides, I'm sick of all these games." I threw Pop's cards onto the ground. "I won't put my fate on any cards, no sir. I'll put them on my actions, and on my friends, and on whatever lies beyond the stars. I'm through with Parsnit, and I'm through with games, and I'm through with bullies, both my pop, and you, Boss Authority."

"You forfeit the duel?" said Boss Authority. "Then you forfeit your blood, both yours and your daddy's."

"No, Boss," I said. "My blood doesn't belong to anybody but myself. No game can give you a right to it, nor my daddy either. I renounce the power of these cards, of this game. I renounce your authority, Boss. I renounce any claim you have to this swamp or its people. I ain't got time for this garbage anymore, and that's a fact. So you can get on out of Marina's Place. She don't want you around, and I don't either. Scram already!"

Boss Authority leapt out of his chair. He flipped the table across the room, and it shattered against the wall. I thought he was gonna rip my head off, I thought he was gonna crush my neck in his palms.

But then something happened, something changed. Boss Authority's ponytail fell from his hair and wriggled on the floor. His teeth fell out, one by one, clattering on the ground like dice. His muscles wilted and his gut sagged. He was nothing without his magic. He was just regular old Bobby Felix, gone wild and strange with power, giving everything that was natural to him away. He lifted his great clockwork fist at me and shook it, but it fell clanging from his wrist.

I could feel it in the air, the spark in my blood, the thunder and boom of my own heart in my chest. I'd done it. I'd out-Orated Boss Authority. The Parsnit duel was mine, and Boss Authority's power was undone.

Marina grinned. "Looks like we have a winner."

Harlen burst into the bar, carrying a bouquet of purple and red flowers in his teeth. He bounded past Boss Authority and Drusilla Fey, dropping the flowers right in Marina's hand. Cecily Bob came chasing in right after him, all huffing and out of breath, his trousers torn to shreds and a big bite mark across his calf muscle.

"Don't let her have them flowers!" he hollered. "Don't let her get a hand on them!"

But it was too late.

Marina closed her fist on the flowers and whispered into them, and when she opened her hand the crushed petals rose like embers above her palm.

"I knew it," she said. "It just took me a second, is all."

The petals turned into a ball of fire, hovering over Marina's open palm. She took a step toward Drusilla Fey, and Drusilla Fey backed away from her.

"Somehow you'd gotten powerful enough to break my

hex and step foot in here," said Marina, "and for a minute I just couldn't figure out how. But it was the stench that gave you away, all that perfume. All those flowers. And I sent Harlen for the one thing I knew could defeat you, could undo every spell you cast on yourself. And Harlen's a good boy, ain't he? He brought them right to me."

Drusilla Fey hissed and charged at Marina. Before she got even two feet Marina blew on the fire in her palm and it erupted in Drusilla Fey's face. Her hair exploded in flames, and snakes fell from her gown, dozens of them slopping, squirming on the floor. She flew out the window, her hair a great red blaze, and vanished into the swamp night shrieking.

Boss Authority—no, he wasn't boss of anything now, so I'll just call him Bobby Felix from here on out—stood there, wide-eyed and vacant, nothing but a little tattooed fella now. He sat down on the floor, just slumped over and hunched there, breathing all heavy. No one quite knew what to do with him.

Pop walked up to Bobby Felix.

"Bobby," said Pop, "I'm sorry. I'm sorry for how I treated you. It wasn't right."

Pop stuck his hand out to Bobby Felix, like he was gonna help him up. Bobby Felix stared at Pop's hand a minute, like he didn't hardly know what it was. That white eye of his was swirling in its socket, and something seemed to be broken deep inside him.

"You're sorry?" said Bobby Felix. "That's what you're saying?"

"Yes sir," said Pop. "I'm apologizing to you, best as I know how."

"Huh," said Bobby Felix, staring at my pop's outstretched hand. "Davey Boy's sorry now." Then I saw a little something harden in Bobby Felix's face, a last flint-spark of meanness glimmering in his left eye. "Well you know what, Davey Boy? I ain't sorry for what I done, not one bit," he said, and whipped a pistol out from his pants pocket. It was a cowardly little thing, as all pistols are, a one-shot popper no bigger than my fist. When it went off I didn't even have time to scream. Pop staggered backward, his hand over his face, blood streaming down his cheek.

"You little jerk," screamed Pop. "You shot me right in the cheek."

"You okay, Pop?" I said.

"It was a weeny little pistol," he said. "Hardly broke the skin on me."

Pop moved his hand from his face, and there it was, the lead ball sticking right out of his cheek like a weird metal tick.

"Does it hurt?" I said.

"Like the dickens," he said.

"Stupid toy," hollered Bobby Felix. "It should have blown your whole durn face off."

He turned tail and sprinted out the front door, but something stopped him in his tracks.

On Marina's dock there stood Sinclair, the Creepy himself, gray and skeletal and skin-blistered, rising up out of the water like the spirit of the swamp itself.

"I come for you, Bobby," he said. "I've come to take you under."

"But you're free," he said, stammering, his voice gone high and mealy. "The hex is broken. I ain't got any magic anymore."

"That ain't gonna keep me from ripping you into little Bobby Felix pieces," said Sinclair. "It ain't gonna keep me from making sure your bones stick in this mud for good."

Bobby Felix hit the ground, and covered himself with his arms. He was terrified, he was, quaking away, like nothing you ever seen before.

"Come on now, Sinclair," said Pop. "That ain't any way to treat our old buddy."

"Do you know the agony he put me through?" said Sinclair. "Do you know what kind of hell I've had to endure?"

"We all been hexed," said Pop. "And we deserved it. Well, everybody did except Marina here. It was our fault, Sinclair. It was our fault we all wound up hexed and cursed and lowdown. We didn't act right, and we got to own up to it."

"But I lost everything," said Sinclair. "The stuff he made

me do . . . I ain't ever gonna be what I was. I'll never be that again."

"You're cured," said Bobby Felix. "The hex is gone. What part of that don't you understand? Leave me be. Just leave me be."

"Cured? Is that what you say? Well, I reject that cure," said Sinclair. "I keep this hex, and I hold on to it for dear life. I'm going down to the depths, Bobby Felix, and you're coming with me."

"But Sinclair . . . ," said Pop.

Sinclair cast a mean eye on Pop, shutting him right up. "Davey Boy, you better thank your dear stars that I don't drag you under neither, seeing as how this is your fault too."

Sinclair grabbed Bobby Felix by the ankle and yanked him into the water. He fought and struggled and splashed, but there was nothing he could do against Sinclair, against the monster that he had become. Bobby Felix's last shouts were choked out by the water, and a few bubbles gurgled to the surface. We watched and waited, but neither of them came back up.

"Sinclair won't kill him, will he, Pop?" I said.

"I doubt it," said Pop. "Sick as he was, Sinclair ain't no killer. Never has been. He'll probably just complain at him for a few months. Maybe make him live off bugs for a while."

"Hope you're right," I said.

"Yeah," said Pop. "Me too."

Up above us a handful of stars fell in long glittering streaks across the sky. Pop bent down and faced me eye to eye.

"I'm sorry, Buddy," he said. "I'm sorry for what I put you and your mom through. I'm sorry for my arrogance."

"I forgive you, Pop," I said, and hugged him.

And in that moment I felt all the hope of love that I'd always had for my pop, the warmth and closeness from him that I'd dreamed of, that I'd wanted for my whole life.

18

BACK IN MARINA'S PLACE, THE chef and the
pianist had come back, and a few of the Baudelaire Quatro refugees were coming out of hiding. I hoped they found
the poor man's head, wherever it was. I hoped maybe he
could get his floating Parsnit house back. I saw Tally milling
around not too far from Marina, like she wanted to ask her
about something. I figured it was about getting cured of her
hex, and I didn't want to interfere. But I still had a question
or two for ol' Tally, so I thought I'd go ahead and ask her.

"Hey Tally," I said. "Whatcha got in your pocket?"

She grinned at me, her spider fangs clacking together. In
her hand she held Boss Authority's Red Bride card.

"Snatched it in the middle of his story," she said. "Can't
believe he didn't notice it, nor Drusilla Fey either. Marina

must have been working some powerful magic on them."

"Or you're just the best pickpocket in the whole durn swamp," I said.

"That too," said Tally, smiling. "I guess this just about makes it official, don't it?" She held the card up, the bright and hideous Red Bride bent on eternal revenge. "I ought to frame this, I should. Hang it up somewhere nice."

"You could keep it here, if you want," said Marina. "It'll be the only Parsnit card I allow in this place."

"Fine with me," said Tally, all bashful-like. "Miss Marina, can I ask you for a favor?"

"Maybe," said Marina. "Depends on what you're asking."

"Well, can you get rid of the spider-folk in me?" said Tally. "Or at least maybe shut it down a little bit? This other witch lady said she could put it in a box and hide it deep down in my brain where it wouldn't bother me anymore."

"Did she, now?" said Marina. "Well, you want my opinion on the matter? Spider-folk is who you are. It's a gift, a rare and beautiful one at that. I certainly can quiet it down in you, but I'm not sure I like the idea of it."

"You haven't had to grow up like I did," said Tally. "You don't know what it's like."

"That's true," said Marina. "Can't much argue with that. Still . . ."

Marina sat there a minute, deep in thought, and if you've ever seen a witch mulling something over, you know you can't help but watch and wonder what's coming next.

"How about this?" said Marina, after a minute or so. "How about you hang around here awhile, maybe learn a thing or two from me. You got magic in that spider-blood of yours, and that's a fact. Maybe if you learned more about your gift and how to control it, being spider-folk wouldn't be such a bother to you. You'd have to earn your keep, of course, and I'd work you pretty hard. But you'd have a roof over your head and three meals a day, and the swamp would be as good as your own. We got a lot of work to do down here in the coming months, and I'd be grateful for the help. After a couple months, you still want your fangs clipped, so to speak—I'll do what I can."

"That sounds okay to me," said Tally.

"Okay?" I said.

"Fine, fine," said Tally. "Sounds pretty great, if you want me to be honest about it."

I stood there, watching Tally, the best and only friend I ever had, master pickpocket, genius pal, genuine lifesaver, maybe my favorite person I ever met in my whole life. She seemed happy, she did. For the first time since I'd met her, she seemed like a person who was looking forward to what came next, spider fangs and all.

Well, that made me happier than anything I'd heard in a long, long time.

19

ME AND POP HIT THE road not too long after. I
wanted to stay in the swamp, hang around with Tally and
Marina, maybe visit the tiny cabin I grew up in, but Pop
wouldn't have it. He said I had to get back to Mom, and fast.
That meant we were going inland, that we were taking an
actual dirt road up, hitching rides on wagons, even slogging
it miles on foot.

That was fine, I didn't mind one bit. I was with my daddy.

And while we rode, and while we walked, we talked.

We talked about everything. I mean it, I got every last
one of my questions answered. Pop told me all about the
last five years, how at first he'd fled the swamp in terror
after Mom begged Bobby Felix to let us free, how he was
convinced there were assassins after him, how he was scared

even to stay in an inn, lest some no-account murderer sneak in and strangle him in his sleep. Pop slept outside, he slept in haylofts, he slept with the horses out in the pastures. A lot of rambling, he did, covering all the Riverlands, even into the Hinterlands and beyond. Until one day he figured out wasn't anybody chasing him, wasn't anybody asking after him at the taverns he stopped in, at the inns where he stayed.

Eventually Pop found himself in Gentlesburg, closer to the Swamplands than he'd dared to go in a year. There was talk of a Boss Authority ruling downriver, but nobody seemed to pay him much mind. That surprised Pop, it did, but what surprised him even more were the Parsnit duels popping up in secret corridors and attic rooms and down-stairs basements all over the city, and not just in the Skinny Yellow Dog either. Parsnit had followed Pop out of the swamp, and he dove back into the game with all his heart. See, Pop had missed Parsnit, even when he was out roam-ing, even when he was fleeing for his life. The cards are like that, he said, they whisper to you while you're sleeping, they call out to you in the night. So Pop got busy playing, only winning sometimes, only winning when it finally counted. Pop was hustling, he was, and all the while he was gathering information.

"I was talking to witches, see?" said Pop. "I was learning all about hexes and how they work, the power of a witch's bond, whether or not it was possible to have one broken. I was doing favors for folks, bad stuff, sordid business, whatever I could to break our witch's bond, to set you and me and my friends free. I wound up in some pretty hairy situations, mind you, stuff I don't dare tell you about. That's just the fact of the matter. But every ounce of my time and energy and heart were spent figuring a way out of this jackpot I'd gotten us in."

He told me about doing a run up north, dashing into a forest seeking bald-headed mushrooms so a witch could curse some governor somewhere. She was scared to go into the woods on account of this nasty hex that made spiders sprout up from the ground every time her feet touched soil. Problem was, the hex extended to folks out there on her behalf. Pop showed me all the scars he had on his legs, all the tiny poisonous bites covering himself.

"I barely got out of that one alive, I did," he said. "And turns out that witch wasn't helpful at all. All she did was say a bunch of witchy things and knock me out with a sleeper spell."

"I got spider bit too," I said. I showed Pop the half-healed wound on my arm, where Tally's granddad had bit me.

"Good night!" he said. "You tangled with that old spider-folk and lived to tell the tale? That's my boy."

He seemed so proud of me then I could have cried. It was everything I ever wanted, having Pop back, traveling with him. It was everything I ever dreamed of.

"I got another question for you, Pop," I said.

"Shoot."

"When I first found you, you were sitting by the river, just thinking all sad-like. What were you doing? Why hadn't you run away?"

"Well, Buddy boy," said Pop, "I don't rightly know how to tell you this, seeing as how it don't sound too heroic, but by that time I'd given up."

"You'd given up?"

"Yep," he said. "I ain't much proud of it, but that's a fact. I'd traveled the whole Hinterlands, the Riverlands, the Swamplands, all searching for a way to break this witch's bond. It simply could not be done. Best case, you could replace it with a new one, but how likely was that? Not very, I tell you. So I quit. I was going to cook myself a big crawfish dinner and eat it and smoke my pipe and wait for the durn reaper to come calling, metaphorically speaking. Then you showed up, and I figured, heck, maybe it ain't all over yet. And I snuck out that very night to get us passage on this new ship they got, runs on steam. It don't care which way the river flows. It could take us anywhere we wanted to go." He shook his head. "Turns out I was a day too late."

"Or right on time," I said. "It seems like everything worked out okay, don't you think?"

"Yeah, Buddy," he said. "I surely do. Even if it was Drusilla Fey's magic that called you to me, all that one-eyed stuff. That's just how magic works, I suppose. No matter who casts the spell, it's got a mind and a purpose of its own, and it wills whatever it wants."

That night we slept under the stars, right out in the middle of somebody's field. A couple of cows mooed and swished their tails. Pop snored hard and loud, same as he always had, same as I remembered from when I was a kid. I lay there and thought about everything, all I had gone through, all the folks I'd met and seen and fought against. I missed Tally, I did. I missed her a lot. I hoped I'd get to see her again. I hoped she would find her cure, or else be happy with who she was. I hoped nothing but good things for her, and that those good things came on her own terms.

I looked over at Pop, his mouth hanging open, that gold tooth catching the starlight. Even though the night was lovely and the moon was high and bright and clear and the stars were like burning angels smiling down, something was bothering me, some sad ugly splinter working its way out of my heart.

I guess I might as well be honest about it.

Even though I told Pop I'd forgiven him, I realized it wasn't so easy as that. You can't just forgive somebody completely in a moment's notice and never feel sad about anything they've done to you again. That's just not how things work. The truth was, I was still mad as all heck about the hex he put on me, how Pop didn't even bother to tell me about why my life was so rotten. I was mad about my blood being gambled away so carelessly, how me and him would both be dead if Mom hadn't pleaded for our lives. I was mad about every durn bit of it. And I guess I'd stay mad, just a little bit, for a long, long time. I was glad I had my pop back, surely I was, but things had changed, and they had changed for good. Pop was never gonna be my hero again. Instead, he was just my daddy—flawed, arrogant, maybe even a scoundrel. I still loved him though, and I would try my hardest to forgive him. I would keep trying, too, no matter how long it took.

That was just the way of it, wasn't it? That's how the world works, how love works. It changes, it grows tougher, it tries to forgive. I don't know how to do it any better than that.

I rolled over in the grass and patted down the knapsack that I was using for a pillow one more time. I tried and tried, but I couldn't get to sleep. So I watched the sky lighten and dim, the stars hide themselves behind that bright curtain of blue, and the sunrise spill over the horizon in reds and golds and pinks. It was like the night was a scrap of paper God lit on fire, like the past was this great big book and God was burning it up one page at a time.

I watched the night burn into the morning burn into the day, and I wondered at it all. Then Pop woke up, smiling his gold-tooth smile, and we set out walking again.

We rode into Collardsville on the back of a wagon full of furniture fresh from market. I was sitting on a stool and Pop had a rocking chair all to himself. We felt like kings, we did, like war heroes returning in a victory parade, riding high above all the townspeople welcoming us home, the hot sun beating down on us, laughing and singing songs all the way.

We hopped off when we came to Mom's street, where the bakery was.

"You ready to do this?" I said to Pop, and he nodded at me, his face all scruffy, his smile forced. I could tell he was pretty nervous to see Mom again.

The bakery was still charred on the outside from the fire, though Mom had replaced the front door and the window frame. But something was wrong. There wasn't the fresh smell of bread wafting through the air, or smoke billowing up from the chimney. There weren't any tarts baking, any fresh pies piping and hot. The bakery looked shut down, boarded up, empty, like not a soul had set foot there in weeks.

I walked up to the door and pushed it open, she hadn't even bothered to lock it.

The front room was dark, and no pastries were set out, just some week-old bread. Flies buzzed around the room, and the whole place stank, like something was rotten.

"Mom?" I said.

"Maybe I ought to wait outside," said Pop, and I nodded at him, because I wasn't sure quite what to do.

I walked on through the storefront, to the bakery, where I'd accidentally set the fire, where the ovens sat cold and unsmoking. And there was Mom, on her knees, her head bowed, like she was praying. Her dress was tattered and torn, the floor all dirty and musty, the burned smell still thick in the air from the fire. Around her were magic things, I knew—balls of twine nailed into the walls, chunks of wood with hearts and triangles and eyeballs carved on them, dead and drying flowers hung in gray bouquets upside down in tiny little altars. If I had ever doubted Mom was a witch, now I knew the truth.

"Mom?" I said again.

She stood up and whirled around, her eyes wide and bright, staring at me like she couldn't believe I was actually there, like I might have been some figment of her imagination. She looked wore out, Mom did, bone-thin and exhausted, her hair a mess of gray tangles, her skin pale and sallow, wrinkles burrowed deep around her eyes. I bet she hadn't left this spot, not for one second, since I ran off. I bet she'd spent night and day praying right here, casting her spells, not ceasing, not daring to quit. Her hand went to her cheek, and for a second neither of us said a word. We just stood there and looked at each other, both of us changed, both of us never to be the same again.

"Buddy," she said, and I burst out crying and I ran to her, and she scooped me up in her arms and held me close, and we cried together, and I knew at last I was home, maybe for the first time ever.

After a minute Mom went still, and I realized that Pop had followed me in, that he was standing behind me, right there in the doorway. She held me tight and got a fistful of my hair and pulled me so close it hurt, it did, and I was scared she'd yank my hair clean out. But then her hand relaxed, and she let go of me. But I didn't let go of her, no sir, I held on tight to my mom.

For a whole minute nobody moved. Then Pop said, "Well, I best be going."

He turned in the doorway to leave.

Mom finally spoke.

"David," she said.

Pop stopped and looked back at her, his face so full of hope and sadness I could hardly bear it.

"Thank you," she said, "for bringing Buddy home."

Pop smiled a little bit at that. He tipped his hat to her. A spear of sunlight caught his gold tooth and it glistened.

For a second I thought he'd stay. For a second I thought Pop would come in and pull up a chair and sit himself down, and we'd be a family again.

But Pop turned and walked out of the bakery, and I heard him start to whistle a little bit, and in my mind I could see the saunter sneaking back in his steps, the deck of Parsnit cards in the knapsack slung over his shoulder, headed far out of town, to where the soil met water and the Wayward River snaked out before him endlessly.

I hoped he'd come back to visit one day soon.

ACKNOWLEDGMENTS

I would like to thank the following people for their skill, bravery, and kindness: Mom, Dad, and Chris, Jess Regel, Andrew Eliopulos, Bria Ragin, Megan Abbott, William Boyle, Phil McCausland, Len Clark, Louisa Whitfield-Smith, P. S. Dean, Mary Marge Locker, Tom Franklin, Jack Pendarvis, and Lewis Nordan. Thanks be to God. And thank you for reading, whoever you are.

Magical books by
JIMMY CAJOLEAS

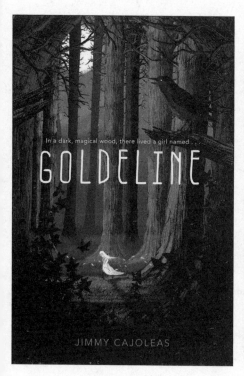

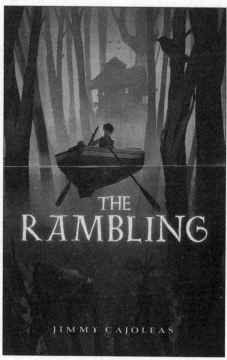